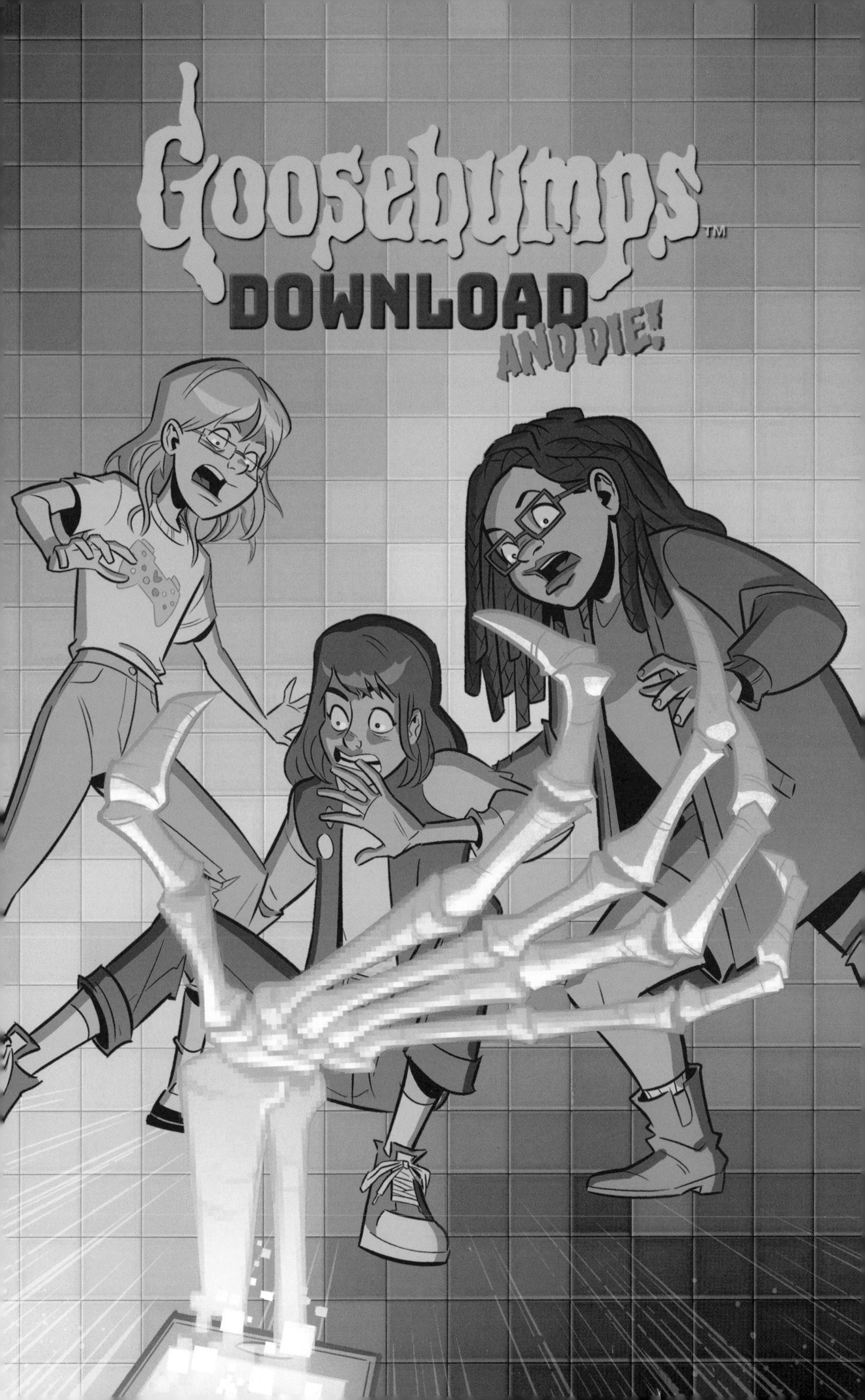
Goosebumps™
DOWNLOAD
AND DIE!

Become our fan on Facebook **facebook.com/idwpublishing**
Follow us on Twitter **@idwpublishing**
Subscribe to us on YouTube **youtube.com/idwpublishing**
See what's new on Tumblr **tumblr.idwpublishing.com**
Check us out on Instagram **instagram.com/idwpublishing**

IDW
www.IDWPUBLISHING.com

Greg Goldstein, President and Publisher
John Barber, Editor-In-Chief
Robbie Robbins, EVP/Sr. Art Director
Cara Morrison, Chief Financial Officer
Matt Ruzicka, Chief Accounting Officer
Anita Frazier, SVP of Sales and Marketing
David Hedgecock, Associate Publisher
Jerry Bennington, VP of New Product Development
Lorelei Bunjes, VP of Digital Services
Justin Eisinger, Editorial Director, Graphic Novels & Collections
Eric Moss, Senior Director, Licensing and Business Development

Ted Adams, Founder and CEO of IDW Media Holdings

Cover Art
MICHELLE WONG

Collection Edits
JUSTIN EISINGER and ALONZO SIMON

Collection Design
CLAUDIA CHONG

Publisher:
GREG GOLDSTEIN

ISBN: 978-1-68405-322-3 21 20 19 18 1 2 3 4

GOOSEBUMPS: DOWNLOAD AND DIE. SEPTEMBER 2018. FIRST PRINTING.

Originally published as GOOSEBUMPS: DOWNLOAD AND DIE issues#1–3.

Special thanks to R.L. Stine.

For international rights, contact licensing@idwpublishing.com

SCHOLASTIC

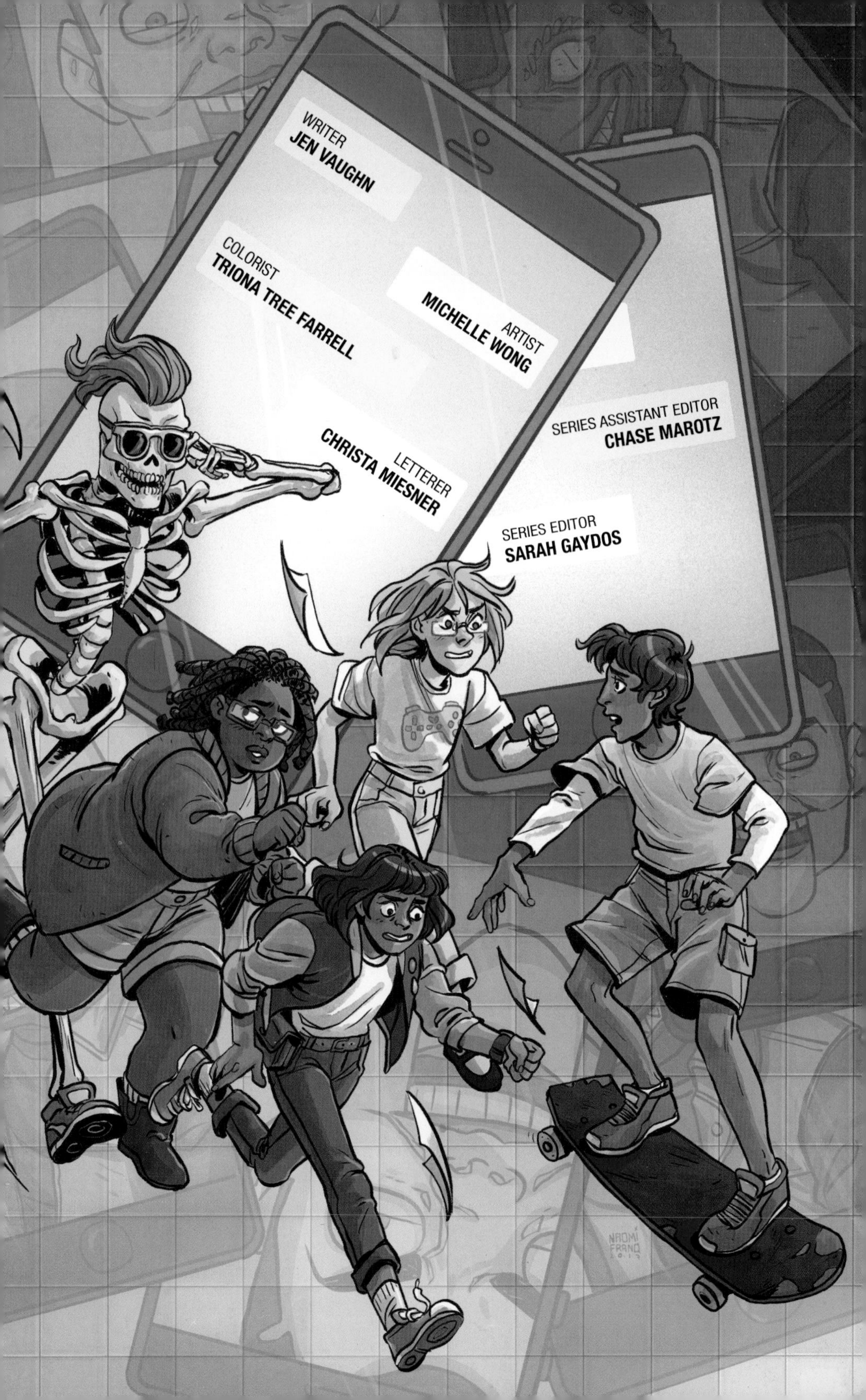

WRITER
JEN VAUGHN
COLORIST
TRIONA TREE FARRELL
ARTIST
MICHELLE WONG
LETTERER
CHRISTA MIESNER
SERIES ASSISTANT EDITOR
CHASE MAROTZ
SERIES EDITOR
SARAH GAYDOS

When I was a kid, I was a comic book freak. I'd spend hours spinning the comic book rack at my neighborhood drugstore, studying the covers and seeing what new titles came in that week.

Sometimes the druggist would chase me away. He didn't appreciate a fanatic loitering in his magazine section. Believe it or not, comics cost a dime back then, and I was determined to be very careful about how I spent my ten cents.

In those long ago days, you could buy a subscription to a comic book and receive it every month in the mail. This made every trip to the mailbox exciting for me.

I subscribed to a bunch of comic books—Westerns, horror comics, superhero books. But one of my favorite comic book categories barely exists today: Funny Animal Comics.

Sure, there were the Disney characters. And the Looney Tunes gang. I enjoyed their comics immensely. But there were others I loved and laughed at and treasured. Many characters mostly forgotten today. *Heckle & Jeckle* were favorites of mine. Two magpies who walked around wearing straw hats and talked like English lords. Then there was *Baby Huey*, an enormous, diapered duck or goose bigger than an elephant. *The Fox and the Crow* were favorites of mine. As well as *Andy Panda* and *Charlie Chicken* and *Chilly Willy* (a penguin).

See? I told you most of these characters are long-forgotten. But for much of my childhood, they brought a special kind of reading excitement.

Now, I'm proud that my *Goosebumps* characters and creations are coming to life in this comic book series. New stories by new writers and illustrators.

I hope *Download and Die* brings you the same kind of reading excitement that I had standing in front of that drugstore rack for hours, so many years ago.

R.L. Stine
SEPTEMBER 2018

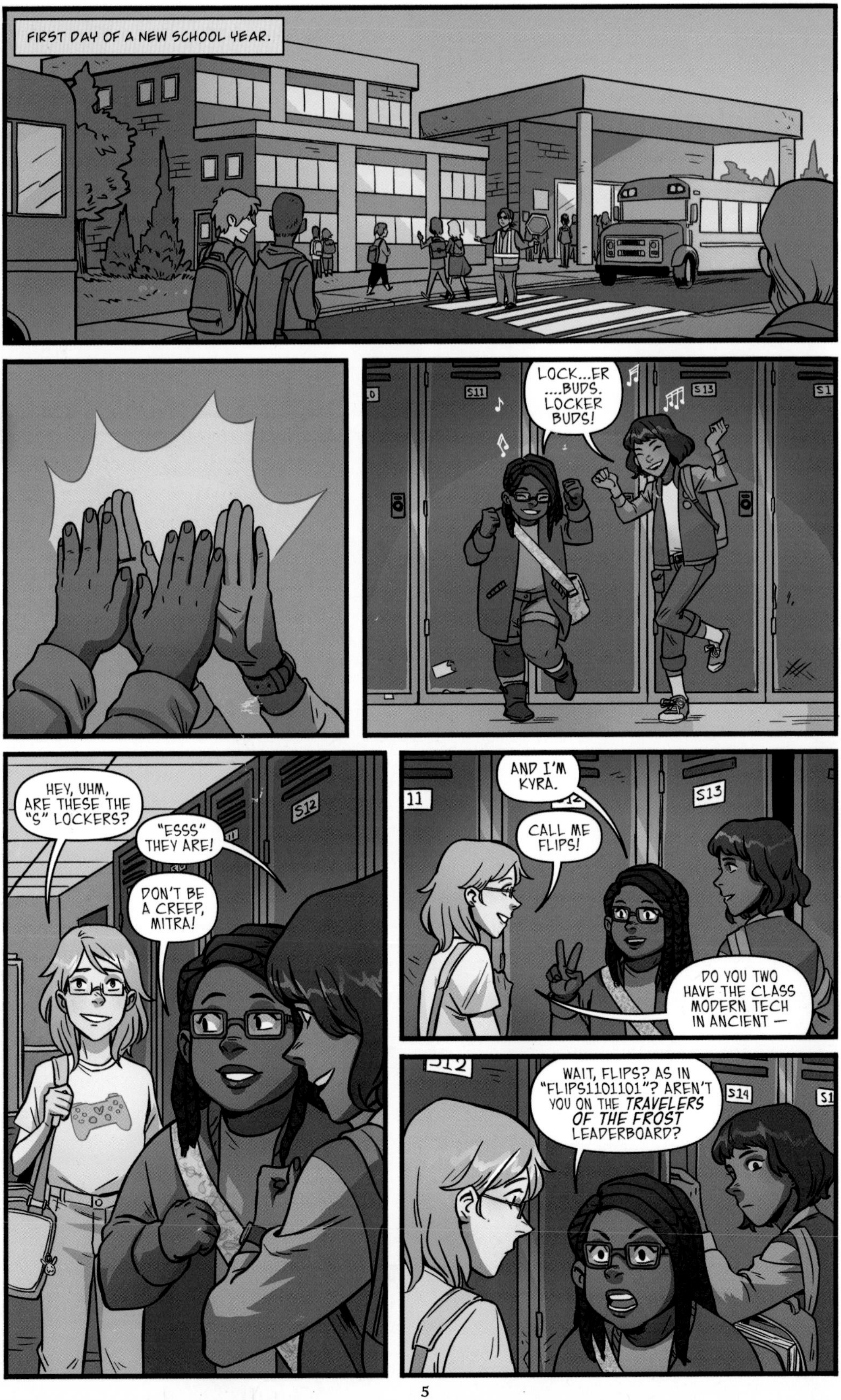

FIRST DAY OF A NEW SCHOOL YEAR.
LOCK...ER ....BUDS. LOCKER BUDS!
HEY, UHM, ARE THESE THE "S" LOCKERS?
"ESSS" THEY ARE!
DON'T BE A CREEP, MITRA!
AND I'M KYRA.
CALL ME FLIPS!
DO YOU TWO HAVE THE CLASS MODERN TECH IN ANCIENT —
WAIT, FLIPS? AS IN "FLIPS1101101"? AREN'T YOU ON THE TRAVELERS OF THE FROST LEADERBOARD?

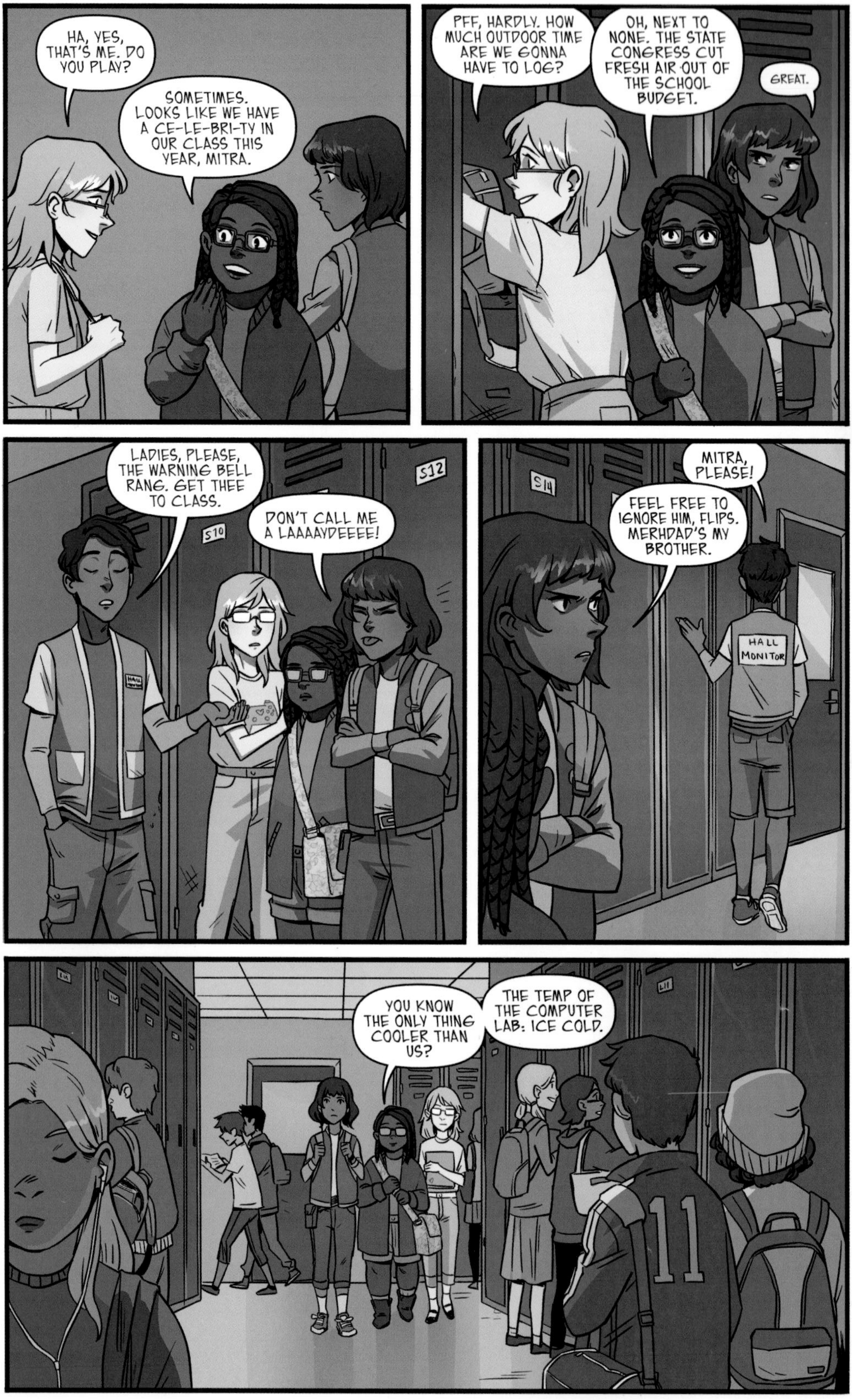
HA, YES, THAT'S ME. DO YOU PLAY?
SOMETIMES. LOOKS LIKE WE HAVE A CE-LE-BRI-TY IN OUR CLASS THIS YEAR, MITRA.
PFF, HARDLY. HOW MUCH OUTDOOR TIME ARE WE GONNA HAVE TO LOG?
OH, NEXT TO NONE. THE STATE CONGRESS CUT FRESH AIR OUT OF THE SCHOOL BUDGET.
GREAT.
LADIES, PLEASE, THE WARNING BELL RANG. GET THEE TO CLASS.
S12
S10
DON'T CALL ME A LAAAAYDEEEE!
S14
MITRA, PLEASE!
FEEL FREE TO IGNORE HIM, FLIPS. MERHDAD'S MY BROTHER.
HALL MONITOR
YOU KNOW THE ONLY THING COOLER THAN US?
THE TEMP OF THE COMPUTER LAB: ICE COLD.
11

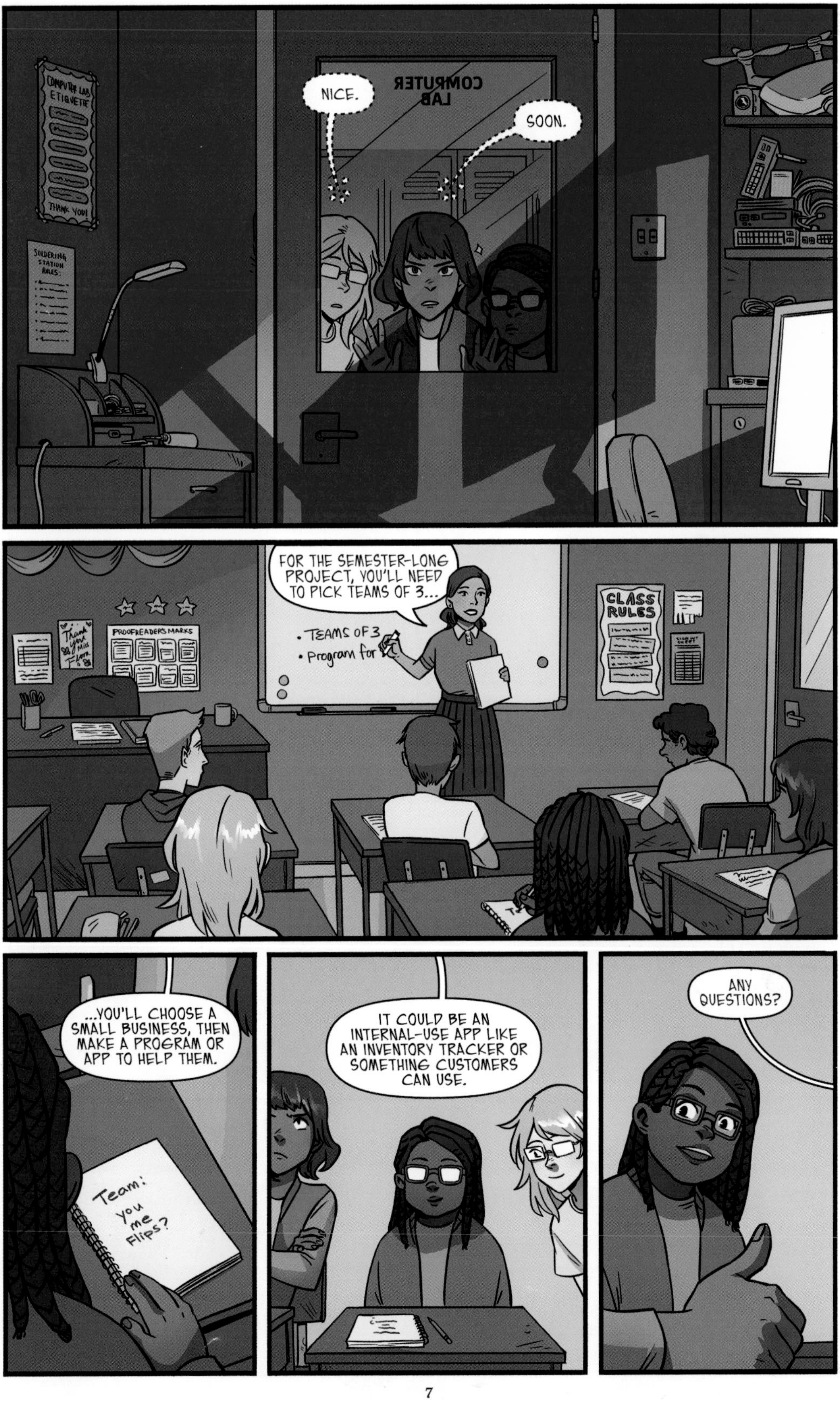
COMPUTER LAB ETIQUETTE
THANK YOU!
SOLDERING STATION RULES:
COMPUTER LAB
NICE.
SOON.
FOR THE SEMESTER-LONG PROJECT, YOU'LL NEED TO PICK TEAMS OF 3...
PROOFREADERS MARKS
CLASS RULES
• TEAMS OF 3
• Program for
...YOU'LL CHOOSE A SMALL BUSINESS, THEN MAKE A PROGRAM OR APP TO HELP THEM.
Team: you me Flips?
IT COULD BE AN INTERNAL-USE APP LIKE AN INVENTORY TRACKER OR SOMETHING CUSTOMERS CAN USE.
ANY QUESTIONS?

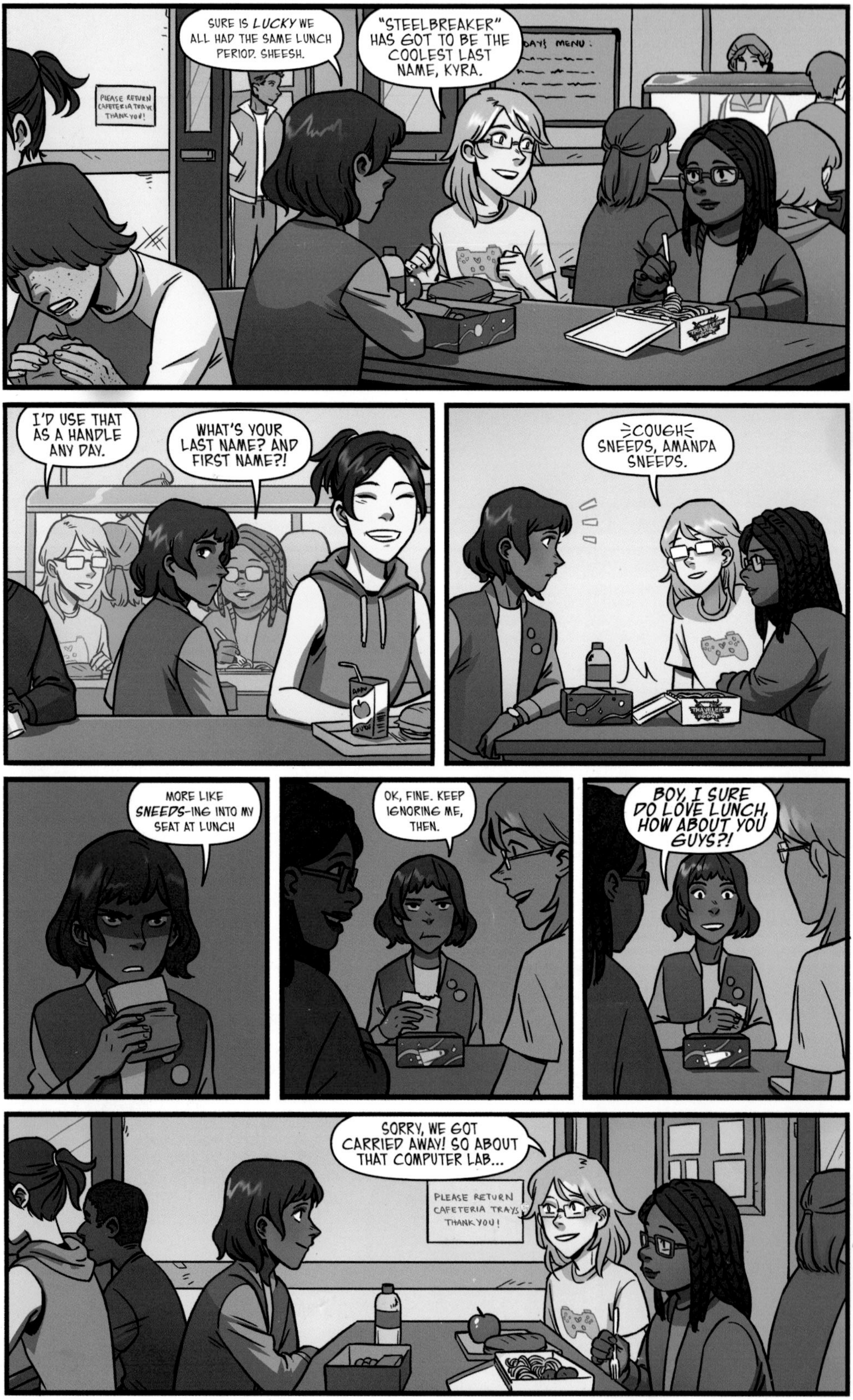

PLEASE RETURN CAFETERIA TRAYS THANK YOU!
SURE IS *LUCKY* WE ALL HAD THE SAME LUNCH PERIOD. SHEESH.
"STEELBREAKER" HAS GOT TO BE THE COOLEST LAST NAME, KYRA.
I'D USE THAT AS A HANDLE ANY DAY.
WHAT'S YOUR LAST NAME? AND FIRST NAME?!
COUGH SNEEDS, AMANDA SNEEDS.
MORE LIKE *SNEEDS*-ING INTO MY SEAT AT LUNCH
OK, FINE. KEEP IGNORING ME, THEN.
BOY, I SURE DO LOVE LUNCH, HOW ABOUT YOU GUYS?!
SORRY, WE GOT CARRIED AWAY! SO ABOUT THAT COMPUTER LAB...
PLEASE RETURN CAFETERIA TRAYS THANK YOU!

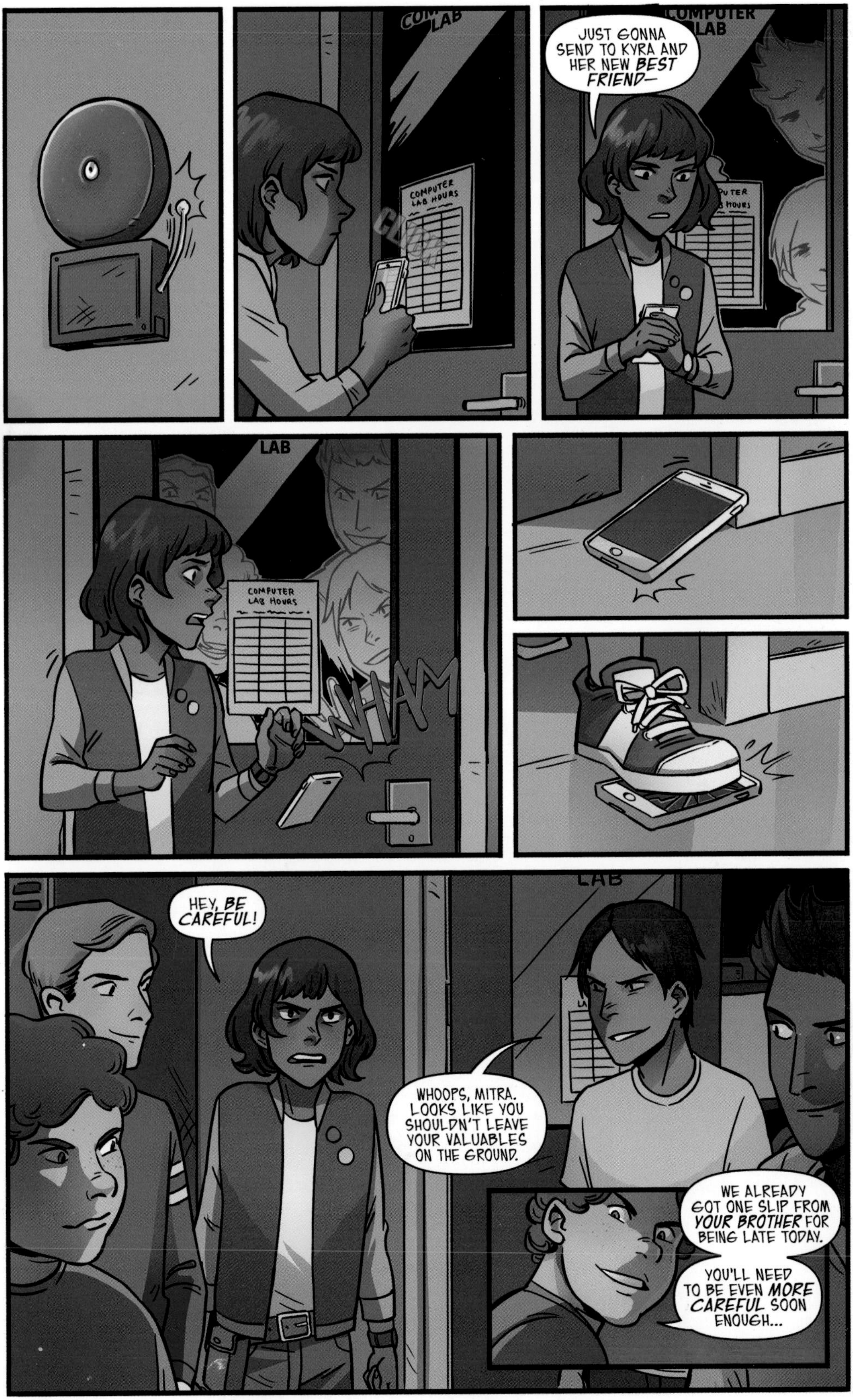
COMPUTER LAB
COMPUTER LAB HOURS
CLICK
JUST GONNA SEND TO KYRA AND HER NEW BEST FRIEND—
LAB
COMPUTER LAB HOURS
WHAM
HEY, BE CAREFUL!
WHOOPS, MITRA. LOOKS LIKE YOU SHOULDN'T LEAVE YOUR VALUABLES ON THE GROUND.
WE ALREADY GOT ONE SLIP FROM YOUR BROTHER FOR BEING LATE TODAY.
YOU'LL NEED TO BE EVEN MORE CAREFUL SOON ENOUGH...

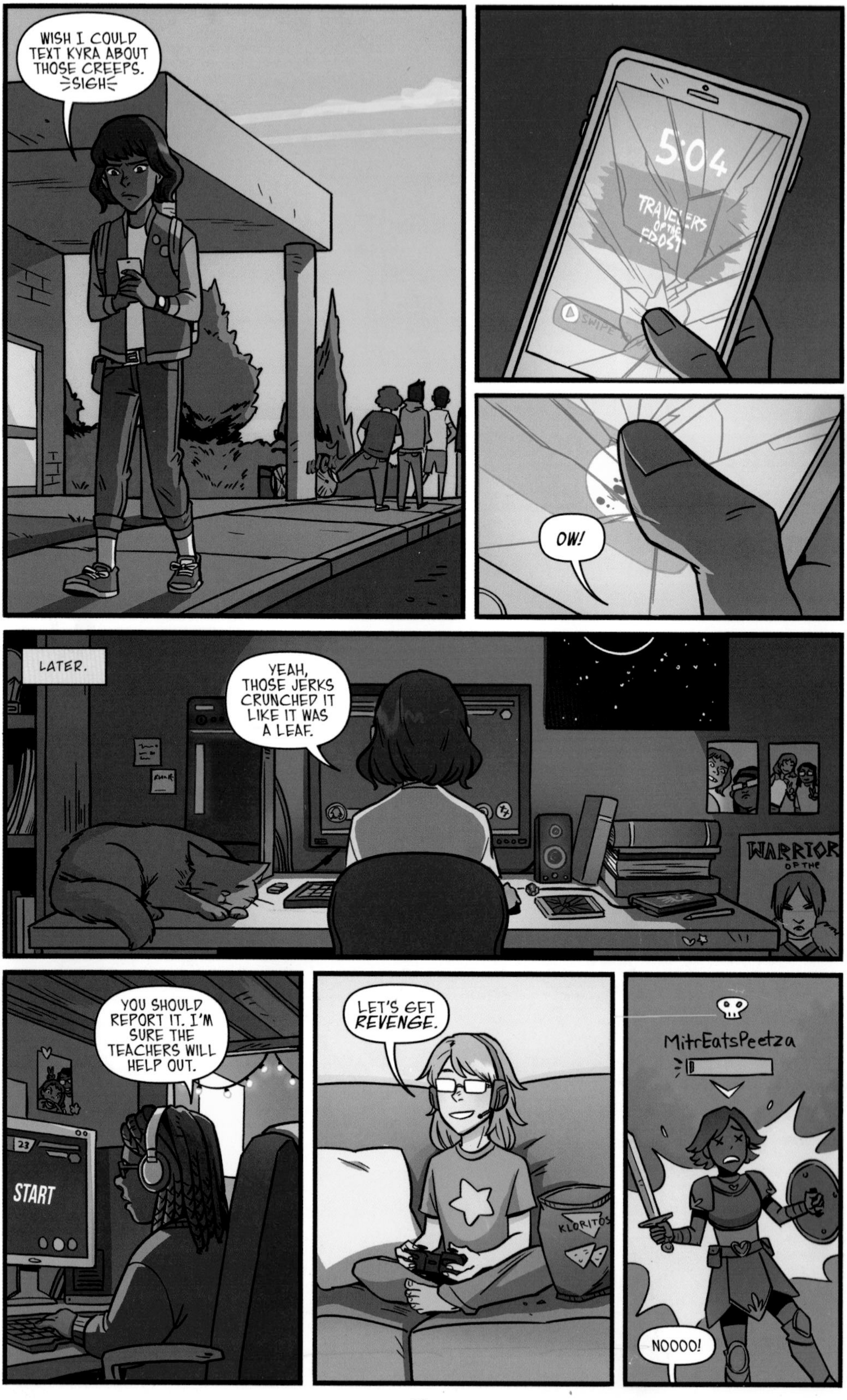
WISH I COULD TEXT KYRA ABOUT THOSE CREEPS. ≡SIGH≡
5:04
TRAVELERS OF THE FROST
OW!
LATER.
YEAH, THOSE JERKS CRUNCHED IT LIKE IT WAS A LEAF.
WARRIOR OF THE
YOU SHOULD REPORT IT. I'M SURE THE TEACHERS WILL HELP OUT.
START
LET'S GET REVENGE.
KLORITOS
MitrEatsPeetza
NOOOO!

FLIPS! I THOUGHT YOU WERE GONNA HEAL ME!

SORRY! I WAS CONCENTRATING ON THE REVENGE PLAN!

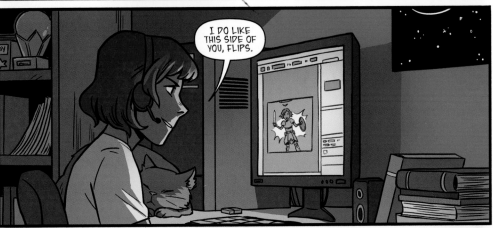

I DO LIKE THIS SIDE OF YOU, FLIPS.

THE TEACHERS ARE THERE TO HELP US, MITRA!

EXCEPT WHEN MY SLINGSHOT GOT STOLEN.

BECAUSE THEY WEREN'T ALLOWED IN SCHOOL! AND WE WERE FIVE!

GOOD POINT.

me when my phone bro

POST

CANCEL

MAN, IF I WANT A NEW PHONE, I'M GONNA HAVE TO WALK A LOT OF DOGS.

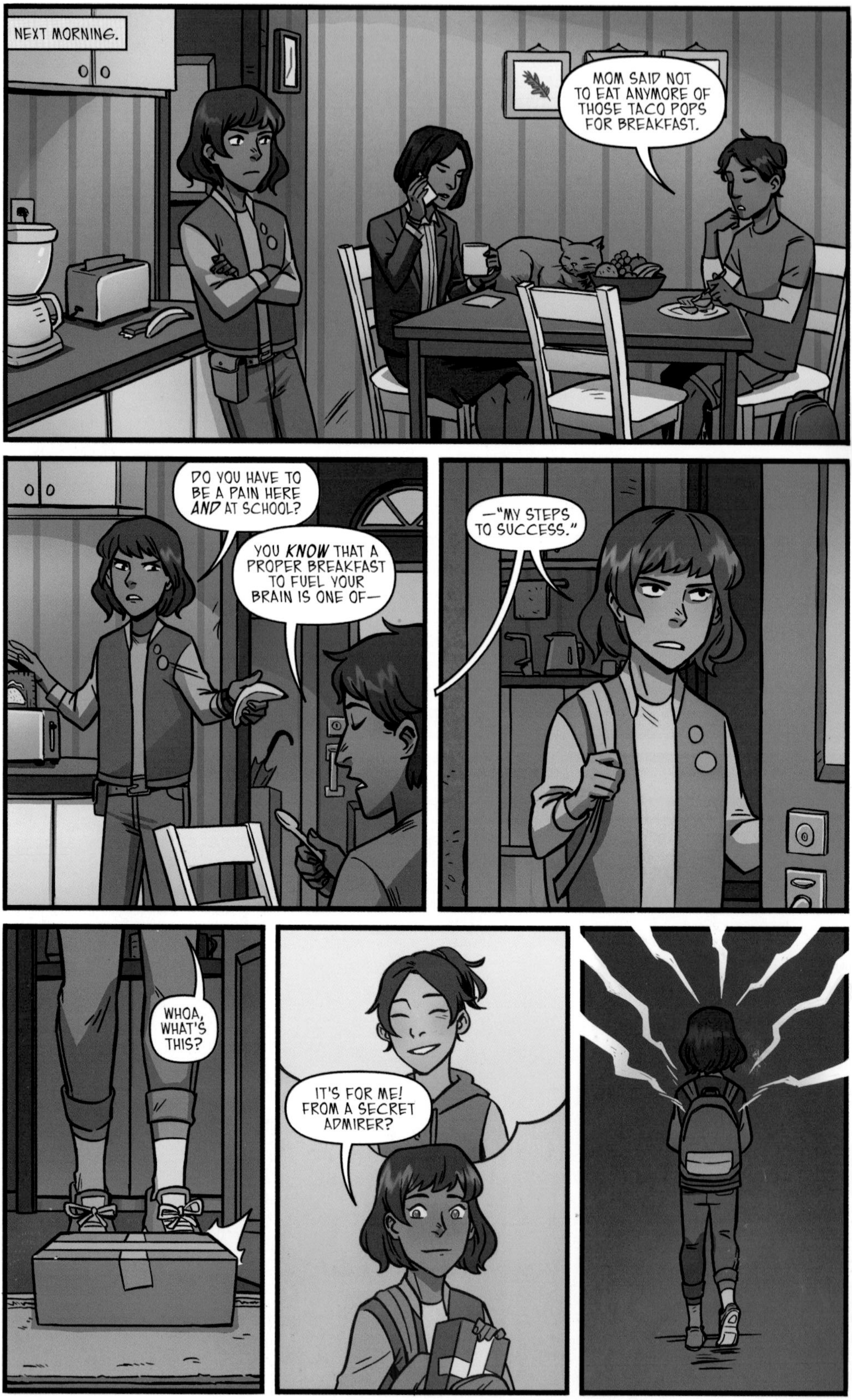
NEXT MORNING.
MOM SAID NOT TO EAT ANYMORE OF THOSE TACO POPS FOR BREAKFAST.
DO YOU HAVE TO BE A PAIN HERE AND AT SCHOOL?
YOU KNOW THAT A PROPER BREAKFAST TO FUEL YOUR BRAIN IS ONE OF—
—"MY STEPS TO SUCCESS."
WHOA, WHAT'S THIS?
IT'S FOR ME! FROM A SECRET ADMIRER?

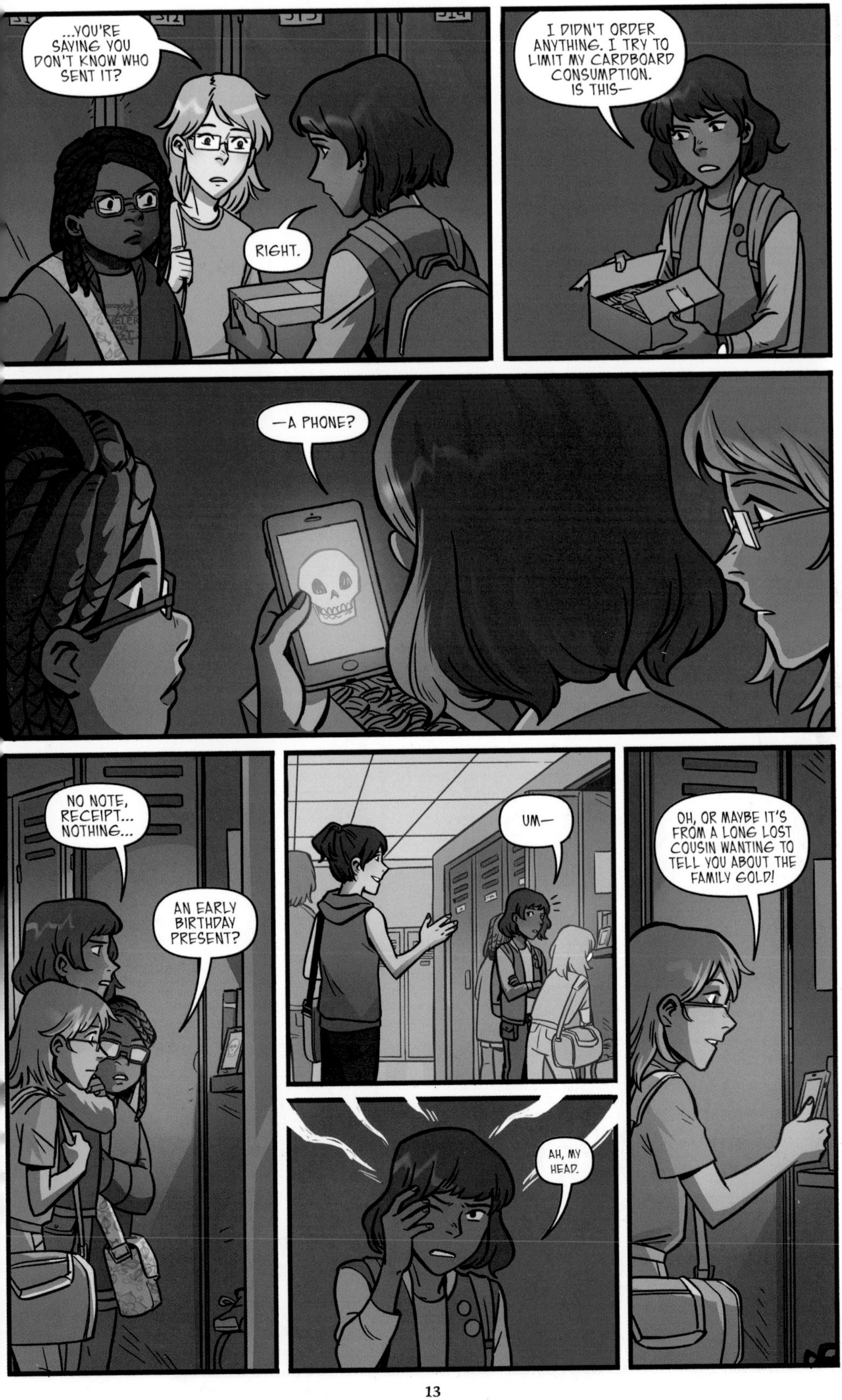
...YOU'RE SAYING YOU DON'T KNOW WHO SENT IT?
RIGHT.
I DIDN'T ORDER ANYTHING. I TRY TO LIMIT MY CARDBOARD CONSUMPTION. IS THIS—
—A PHONE?
NO NOTE, RECEIPT... NOTHING...
AN EARLY BIRTHDAY PRESENT?
UM—
AH, MY HEAD.
OH, OR MAYBE IT'S FROM A LONG LOST COUSIN WANTING TO TELL YOU ABOUT THE FAMILY GOLD!

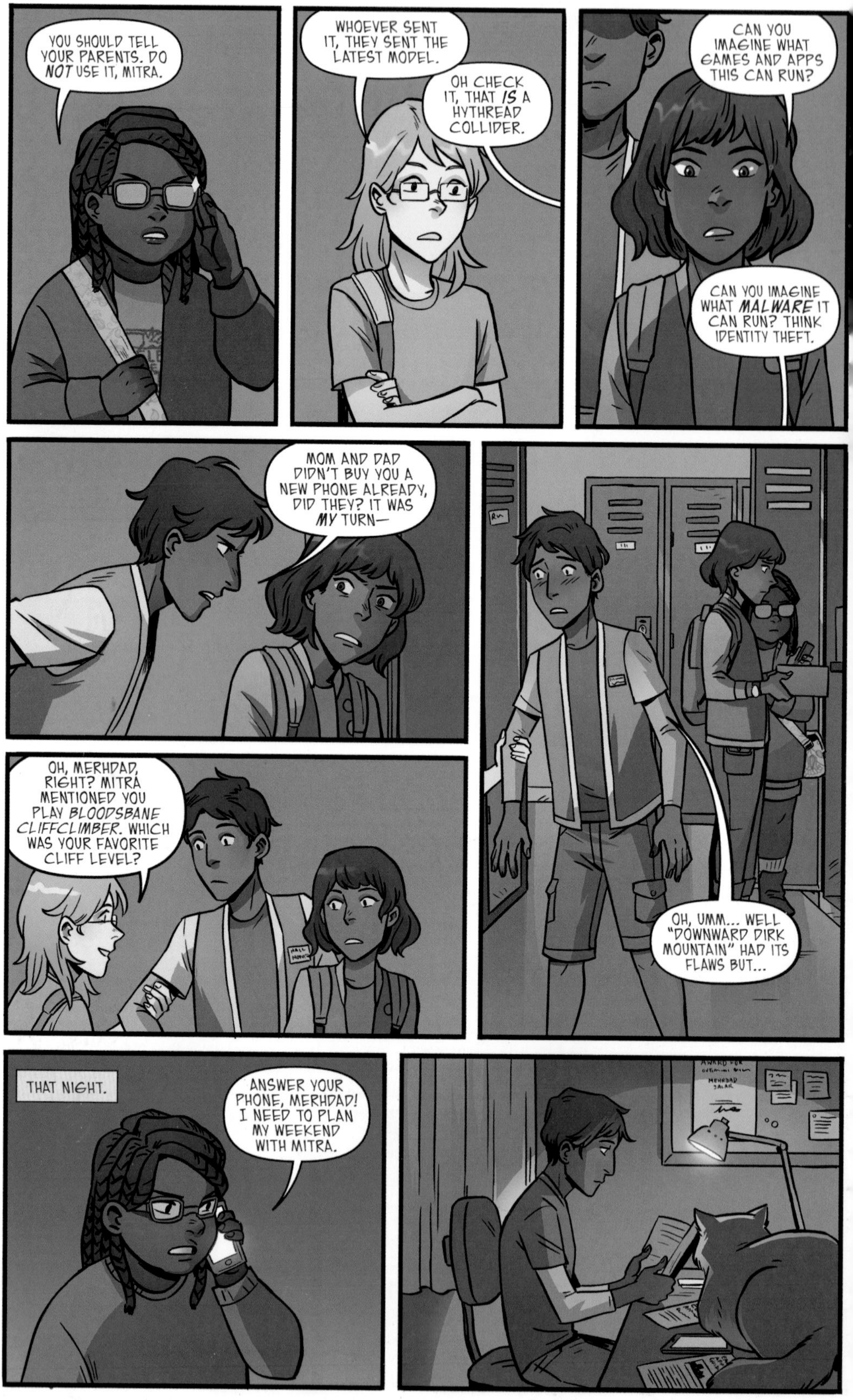
YOU SHOULD TELL YOUR PARENTS. DO NOT USE IT, MITRA.
WHOEVER SENT IT, THEY SENT THE LATEST MODEL.
OH CHECK IT, THAT IS A HYTHREAD COLLIDER.
CAN YOU IMAGINE WHAT GAMES AND APPS THIS CAN RUN?
CAN YOU IMAGINE WHAT MALWARE IT CAN RUN? THINK IDENTITY THEFT.
MOM AND DAD DIDN'T BUY YOU A NEW PHONE ALREADY, DID THEY? IT WAS MY TURN—
OH, MERHDAD, RIGHT? MITRA MENTIONED YOU PLAY BLOODSBANE CLIFFCLIMBER. WHICH WAS YOUR FAVORITE CLIFF LEVEL?
OH, UMM... WELL "DOWNWARD DIRK MOUNTAIN" HAD ITS FLAWS BUT...
THAT NIGHT.
ANSWER YOUR PHONE, MERHDAD! I NEED TO PLAN MY WEEKEND WITH MITRA.

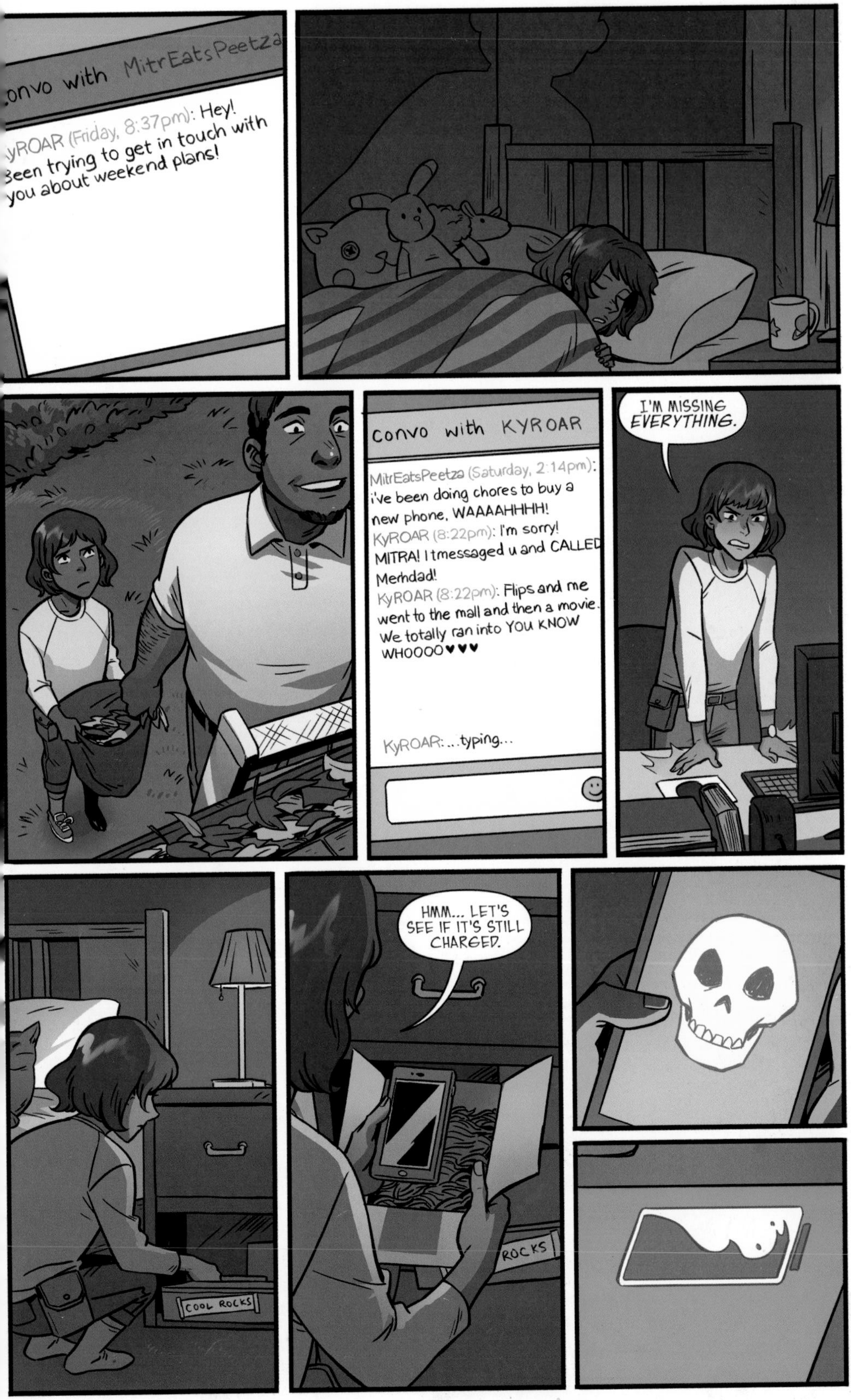
Convo with MitrEatsPeetza
KyROAR (Friday, 8:37pm): Hey! Been trying to get in touch with you about weekend plans!
Convo with KYROAR
MitrEatsPeetza (Saturday, 2:14pm): i've been doing chores to buy a new phone, WAAAAHHHH!
KyROAR (8:22pm): I'm sorry! MITRA! I tmessaged u and CALLED Merhdad!
KyROAR (8:22pm): Flips and me went to the mall and then a movie. We totally ran into YOU KNOW WHOOOO♥♥♥
KyROAR: ...typing...
I'M MISSING EVERYTHING.
COOL ROCKS
HMM... LET'S SEE IF IT'S STILL CHARGED.
ROCKS

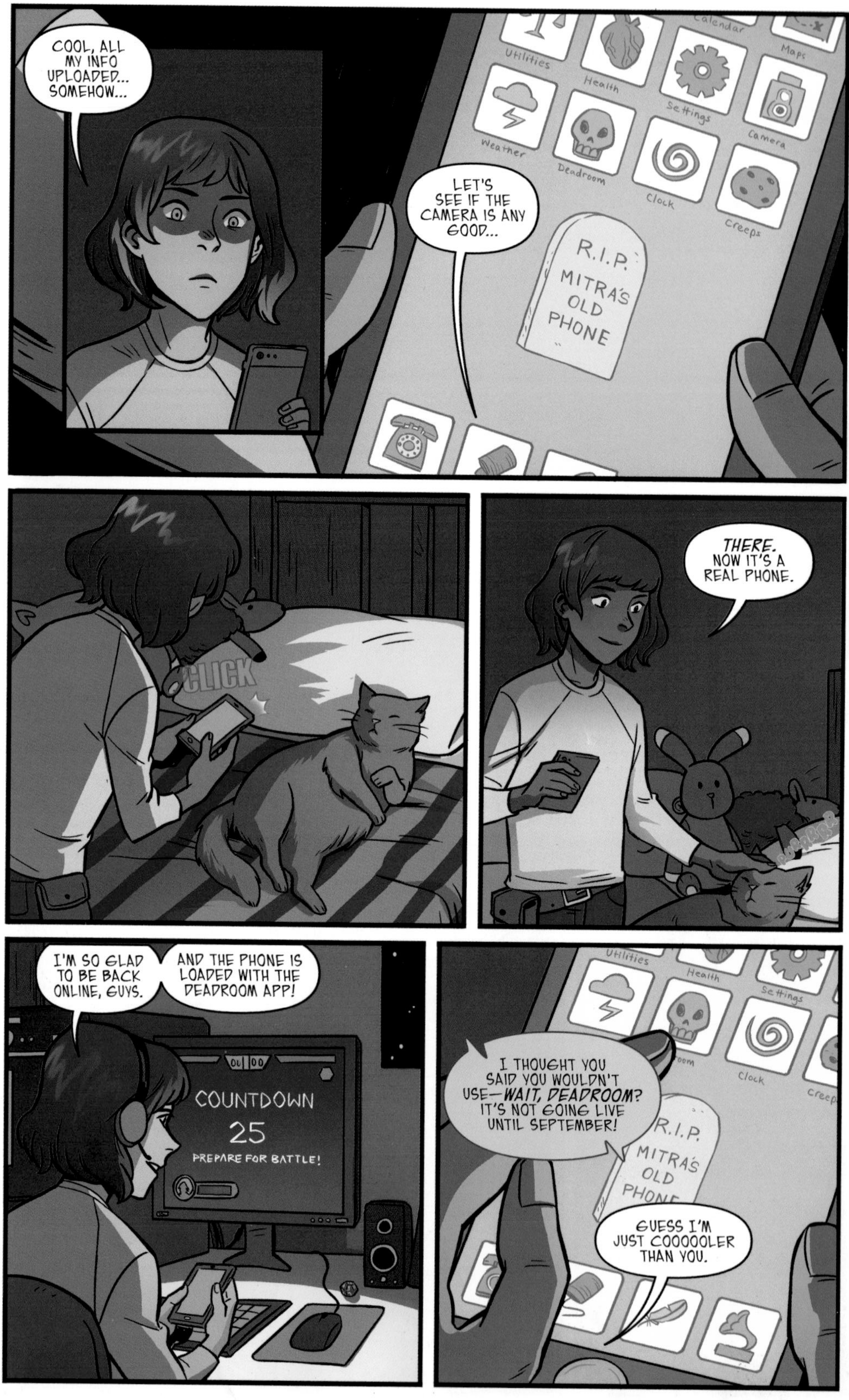
COOL, ALL MY INFO UPLOADED... SOMEHOW...
Utilities
Health
Calendar
Maps
Settings
Camera
Weather
Deadroom
Clock
Creeps
LET'S SEE IF THE CAMERA IS ANY GOOD...
R.I.P. MITRA'S OLD PHONE
CLICK
THERE. NOW IT'S A REAL PHONE.
I'M SO GLAD TO BE BACK ONLINE, GUYS.
AND THE PHONE IS LOADED WITH THE DEADROOM APP!
COUNTDOWN
25
PREPARE FOR BATTLE!
I THOUGHT YOU SAID YOU WOULDN'T USE—WAIT, DEADROOM? IT'S NOT GOING LIVE UNTIL SEPTEMBER!
GUESS I'M JUST COOOOOLER THAN YOU.

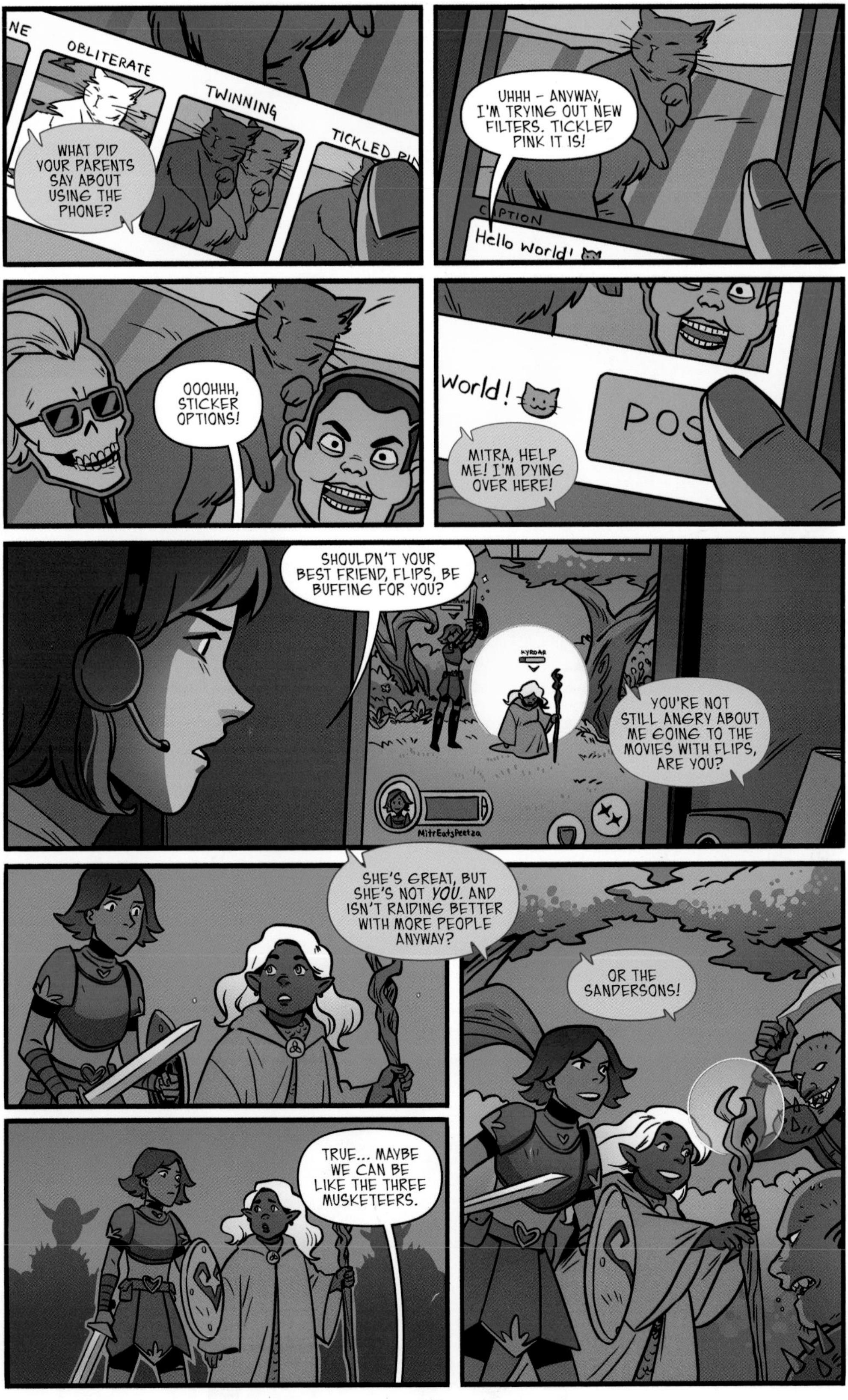
NE
OBLITERATE
TWINNING
TICKLED PI
WHAT DID YOUR PARENTS SAY ABOUT USING THE PHONE?
UHHH – ANYWAY, I'M TRYING OUT NEW FILTERS. TICKLED PINK IT IS!
CAPTION
Hello world!
OOOHHH, STICKER OPTIONS!
world!
POS
MITRA, HELP ME! I'M DYING OVER HERE!
SHOULDN'T YOUR BEST FRIEND, FLIPS, BE BUFFING FOR YOU?
YOU'RE NOT STILL ANGRY ABOUT ME GOING TO THE MOVIES WITH FLIPS, ARE YOU?
MitrEatsPeetza
SHE'S GREAT, BUT SHE'S NOT *YOU*. AND ISN'T RAIDING BETTER WITH MORE PEOPLE ANYWAY?
OR THE SANDERSONS!
TRUE... MAYBE WE CAN BE LIKE THE THREE MUSKETEERS.

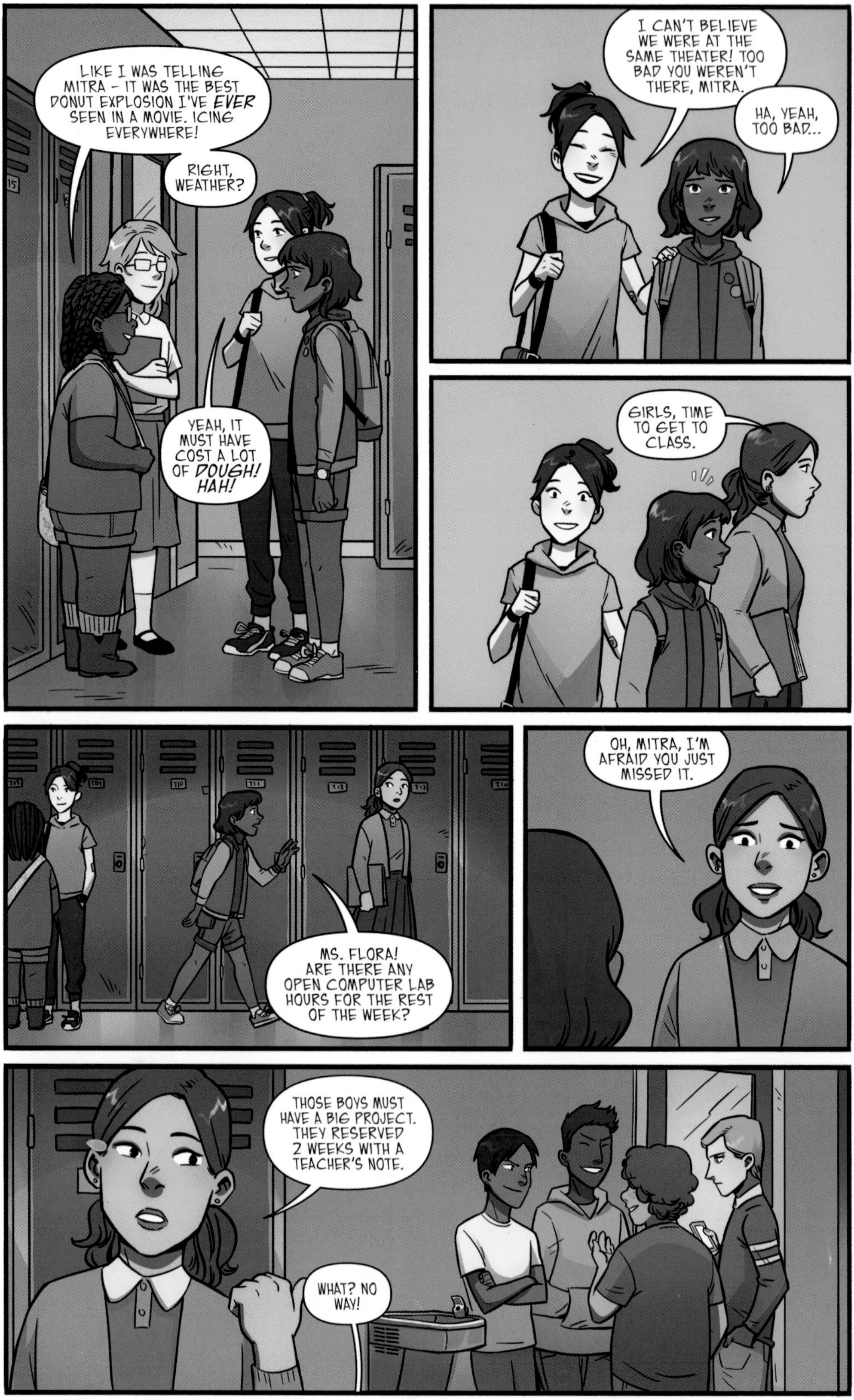
LIKE I WAS TELLING MITRA – IT WAS THE BEST DONUT EXPLOSION I'VE EVER SEEN IN A MOVIE. ICING EVERYWHERE!
RIGHT, WEATHER?
YEAH, IT MUST HAVE COST A LOT OF DOUGH! HAH!
I CAN'T BELIEVE WE WERE AT THE SAME THEATER! TOO BAD YOU WEREN'T THERE, MITRA.
HA, YEAH, TOO BAD...
GIRLS, TIME TO GET TO CLASS.
MS. FLORA! ARE THERE ANY OPEN COMPUTER LAB HOURS FOR THE REST OF THE WEEK?
OH, MITRA, I'M AFRAID YOU JUST MISSED IT.
THOSE BOYS MUST HAVE A BIG PROJECT. THEY RESERVED 2 WEEKS WITH A TEACHER'S NOTE.
WHAT? NO WAY!

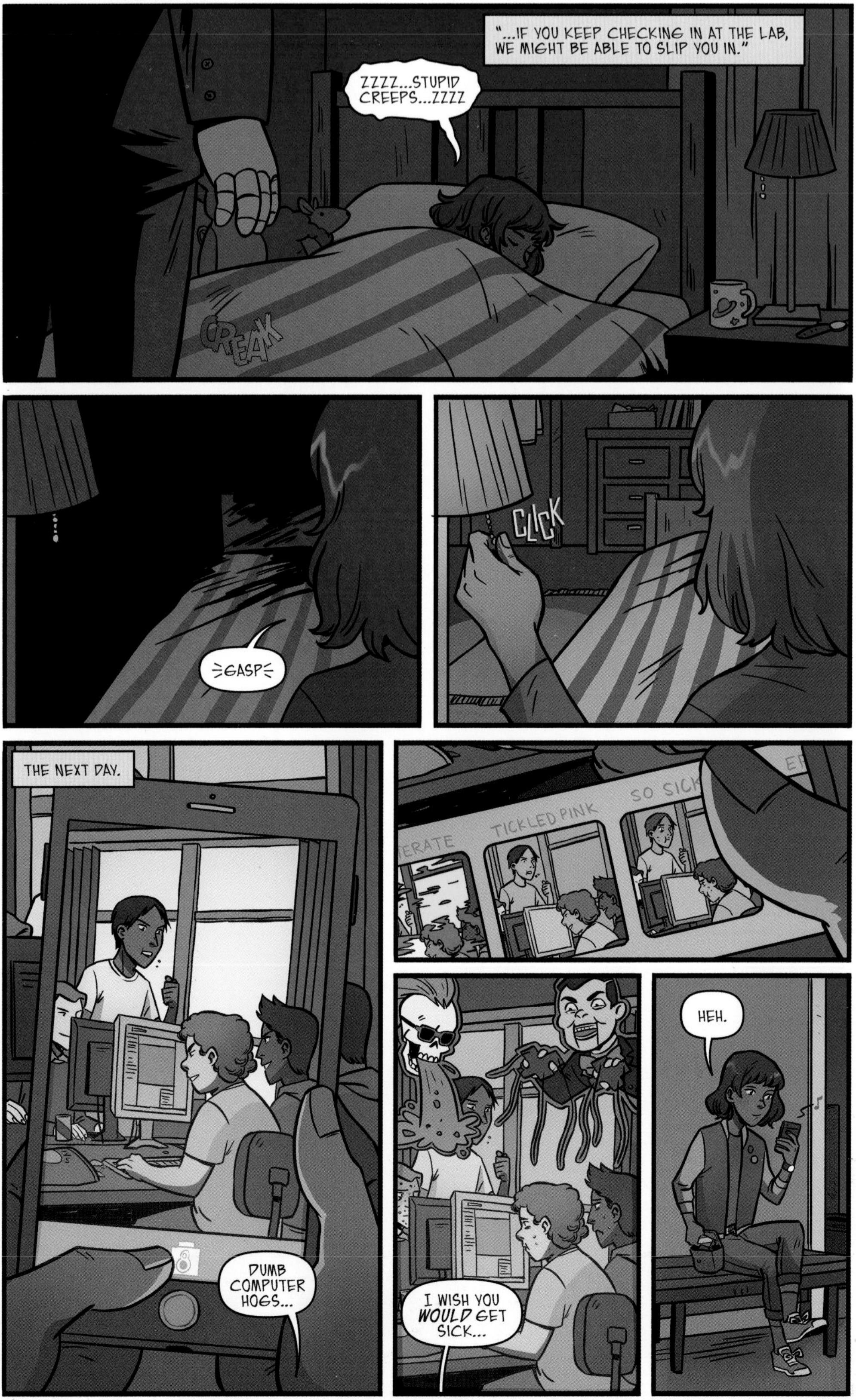
"...IF YOU KEEP CHECKING IN AT THE LAB, WE MIGHT BE ABLE TO SLIP YOU IN."
ZZZZ...STUPID CREEPS...ZZZZ
CREAK
GASP
CLICK
THE NEXT DAY.
SO SICK
TICKLED PINK
DUMB COMPUTER HOGS...
I WISH YOU *WOULD* GET SICK...
HEH.

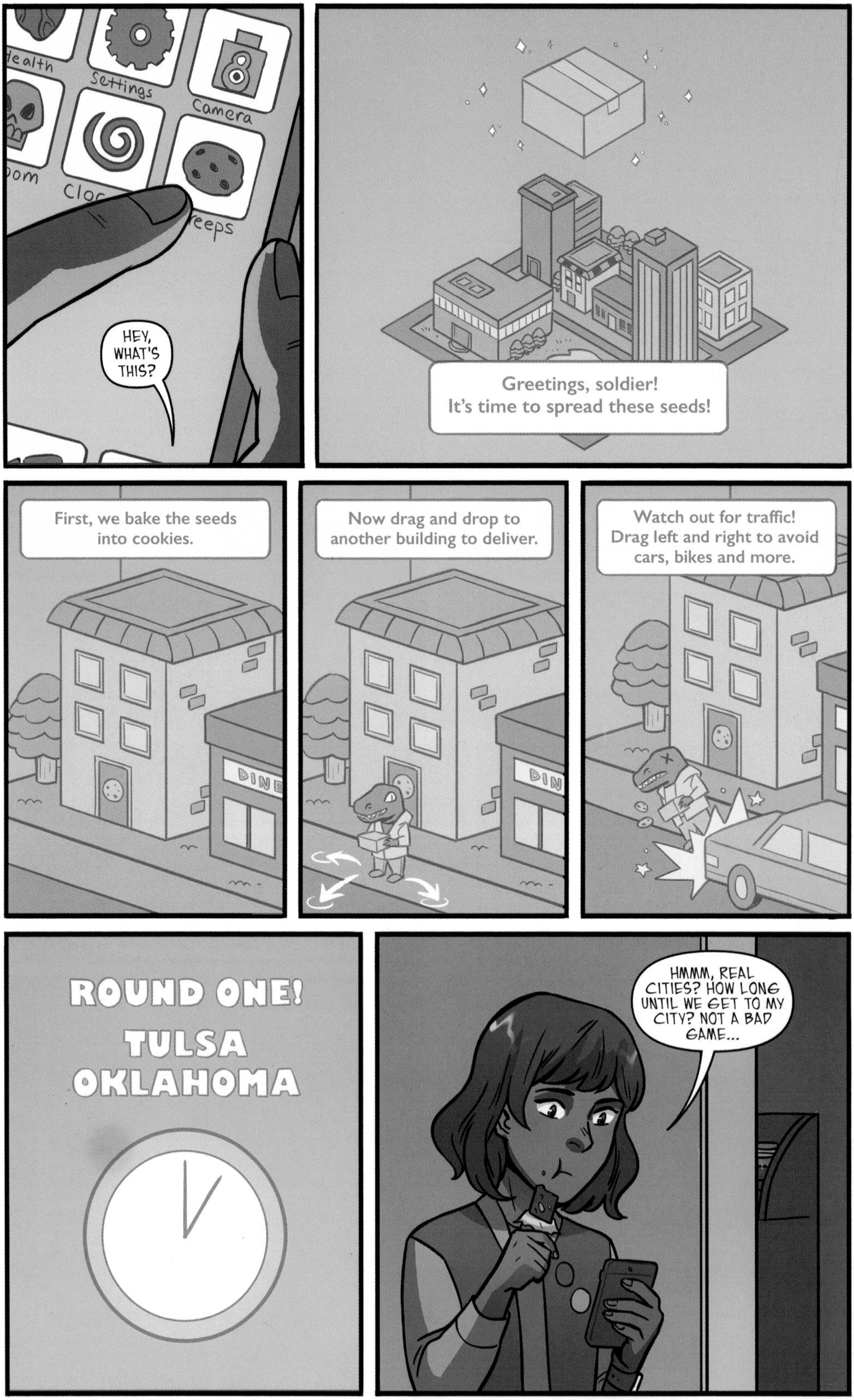
Health
Settings
Camera
Creeps
HEY, WHAT'S THIS?
Greetings, soldier!
It's time to spread these seeds!
First, we bake the seeds into cookies.
Now drag and drop to another building to deliver.
Watch out for traffic! Drag left and right to avoid cars, bikes and more.
ROUND ONE!
TULSA OKLAHOMA
HMMM, REAL CITIES? HOW LONG UNTIL WE GET TO MY CITY? NOT A BAD GAME...

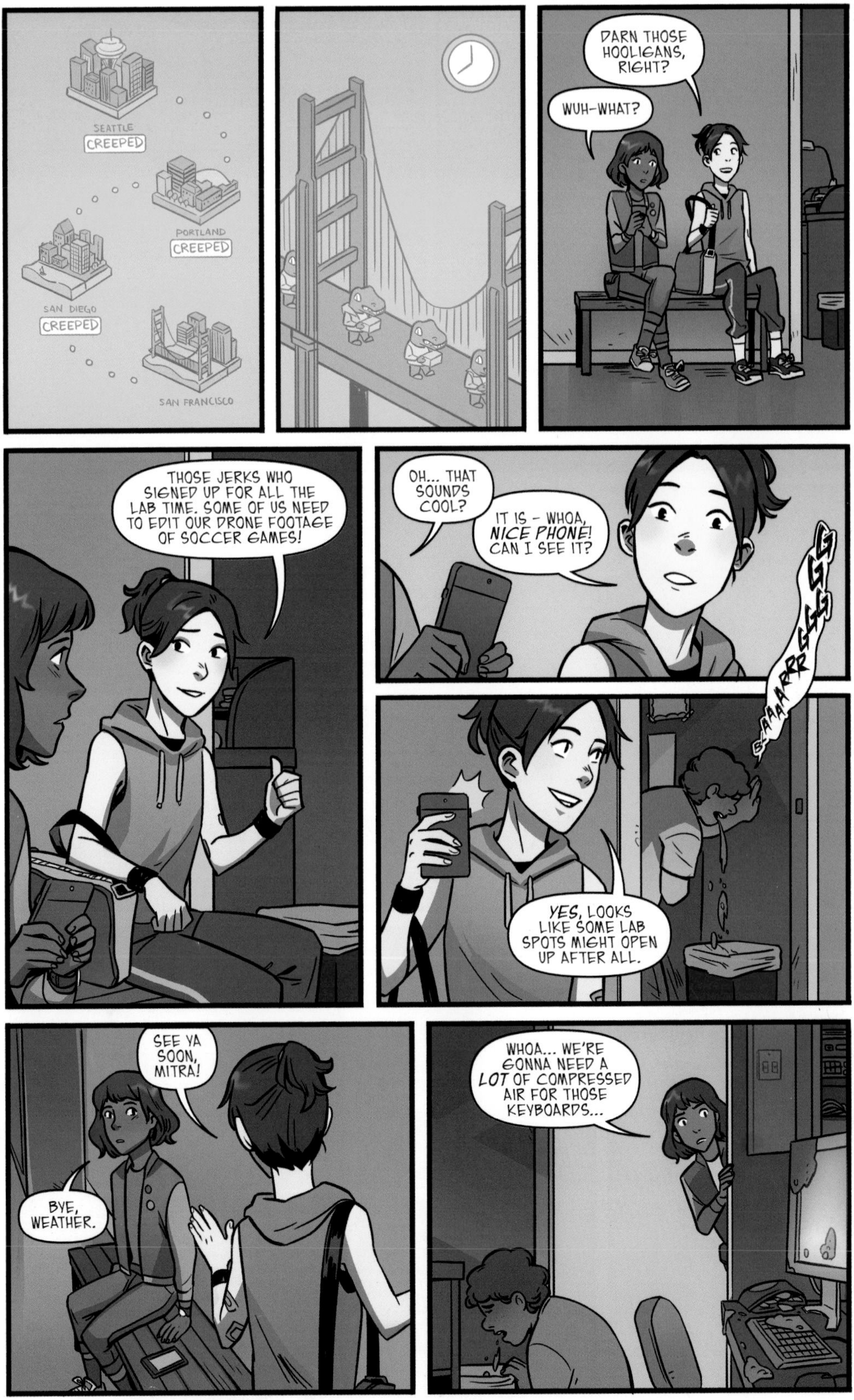
SEATTLE
CREEPED
PORTLAND
CREEPED
SAN DIEGO
CREEPED
SAN FRANCISCO
DARN THOSE HOOLIGANS, RIGHT?
WUH-WHAT?
THOSE JERKS WHO SIGNED UP FOR ALL THE LAB TIME. SOME OF US NEED TO EDIT OUR DRONE FOOTAGE OF SOCCER GAMES!
OH... THAT SOUNDS COOL?
IT IS - WHOA, NICE PHONE! CAN I SEE IT?
B-AAAARRRGGGGG
YES, LOOKS LIKE SOME LAB SPOTS MIGHT OPEN UP AFTER ALL.
SEE YA SOON, MITRA!
BYE, WEATHER.
WHOA... WE'RE GONNA NEED A LOT OF COMPRESSED AIR FOR THOSE KEYBOARDS...

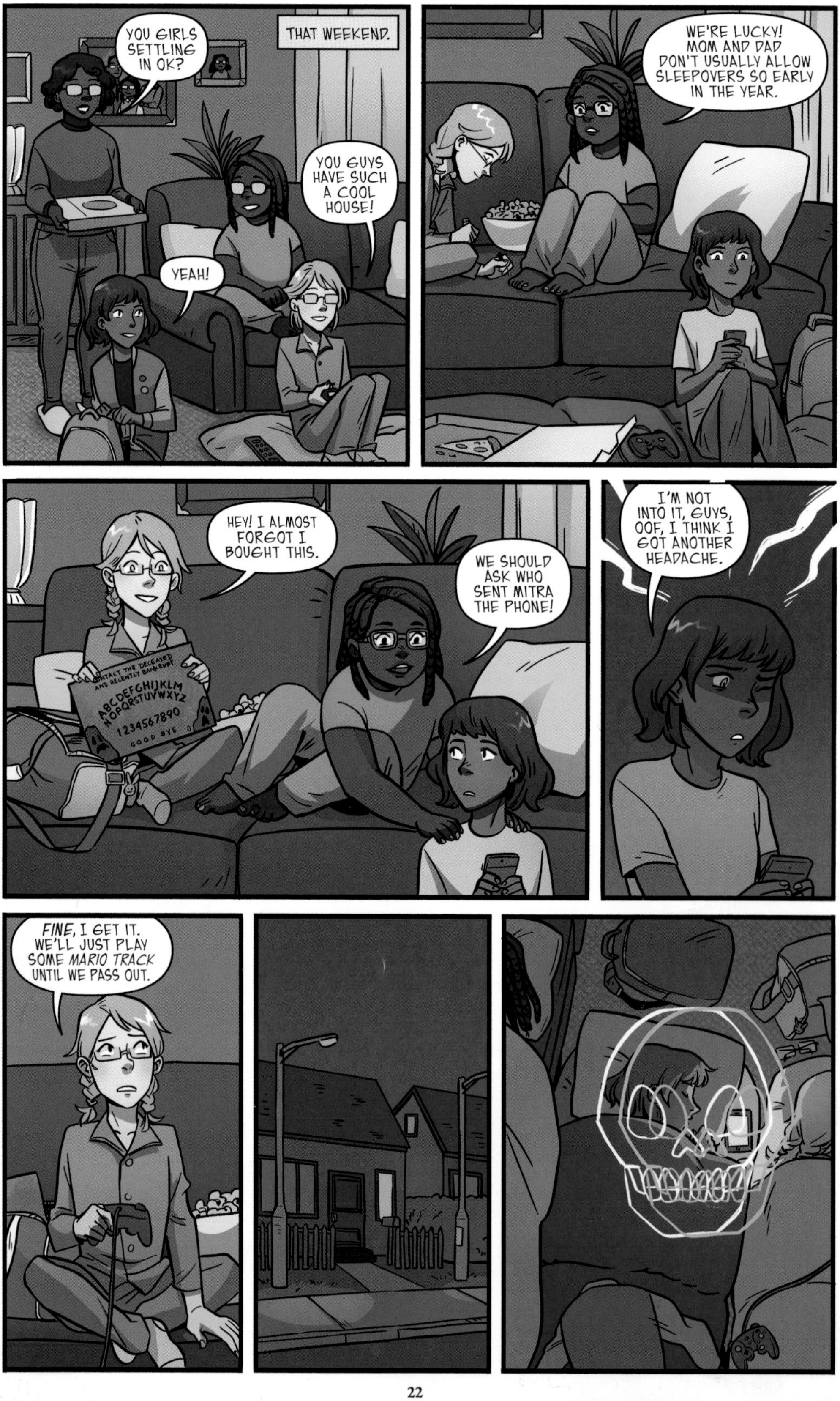

THAT WEEKEND.
YOU GIRLS SETTLING IN OK?
YOU GUYS HAVE SUCH A COOL HOUSE!
YEAH!
WE'RE LUCKY! MOM AND DAD DON'T USUALLY ALLOW SLEEPOVERS SO EARLY IN THE YEAR.
HEY! I ALMOST FORGOT I BOUGHT THIS.
AND RECENTLY BANKRUPT
ABCDEFGHIJKLM
NOPQRSTUVWXYZ
1234567890
GOOD BYE
WE SHOULD ASK WHO SENT MITRA THE PHONE!
I'M NOT INTO IT, GUYS, OOF, I THINK I GOT ANOTHER HEADACHE.
FINE, I GET IT. WE'LL JUST PLAY SOME *MARIO TRACK* UNTIL WE PASS OUT.

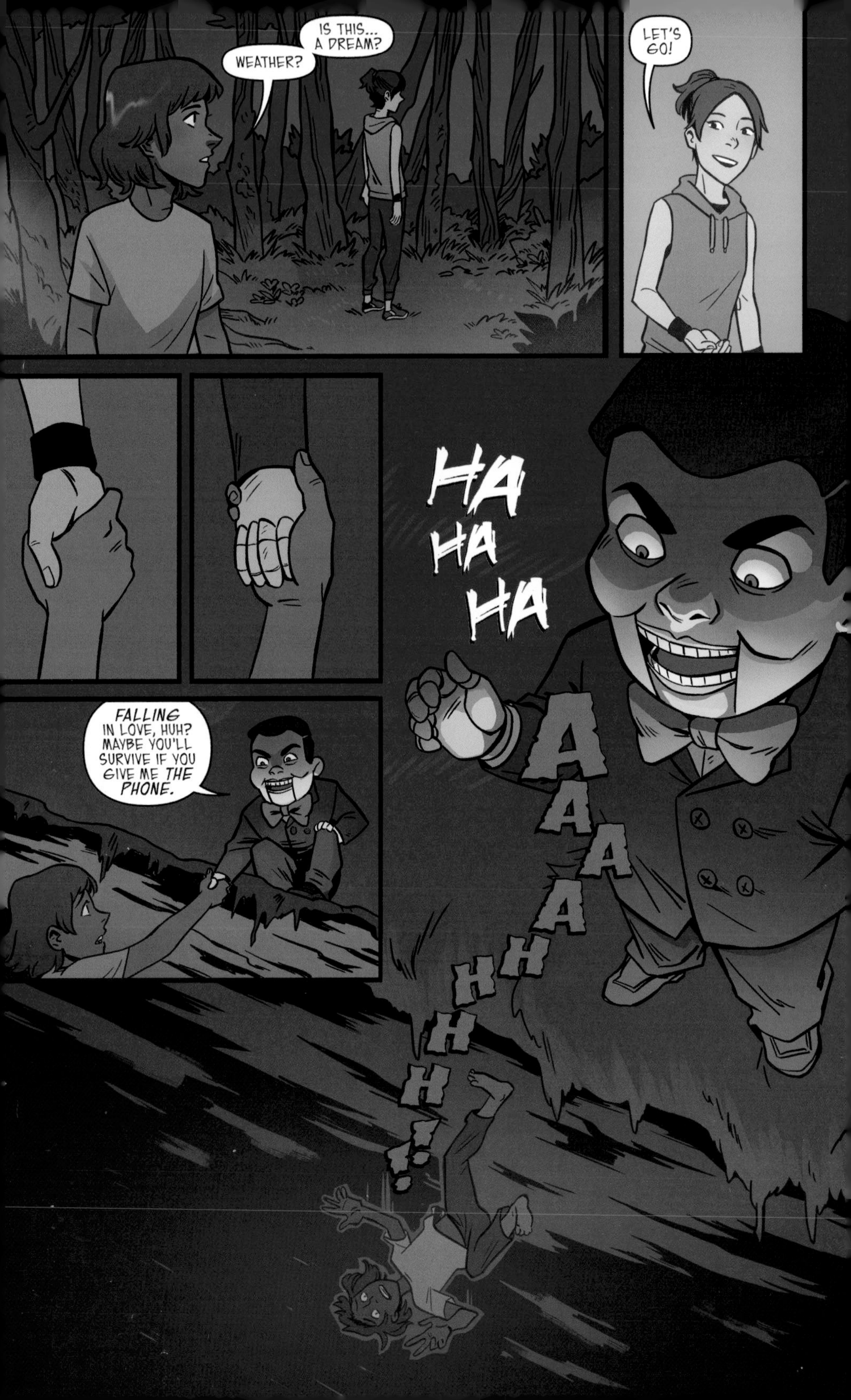
WEATHER?
IS THIS... A DREAM?
LET'S GO!
FALLING IN LOVE, HUH? MAYBE YOU'LL SURVIVE IF YOU GIVE ME THE PHONE.
HA HA HA
AAAAAHHHHH!!

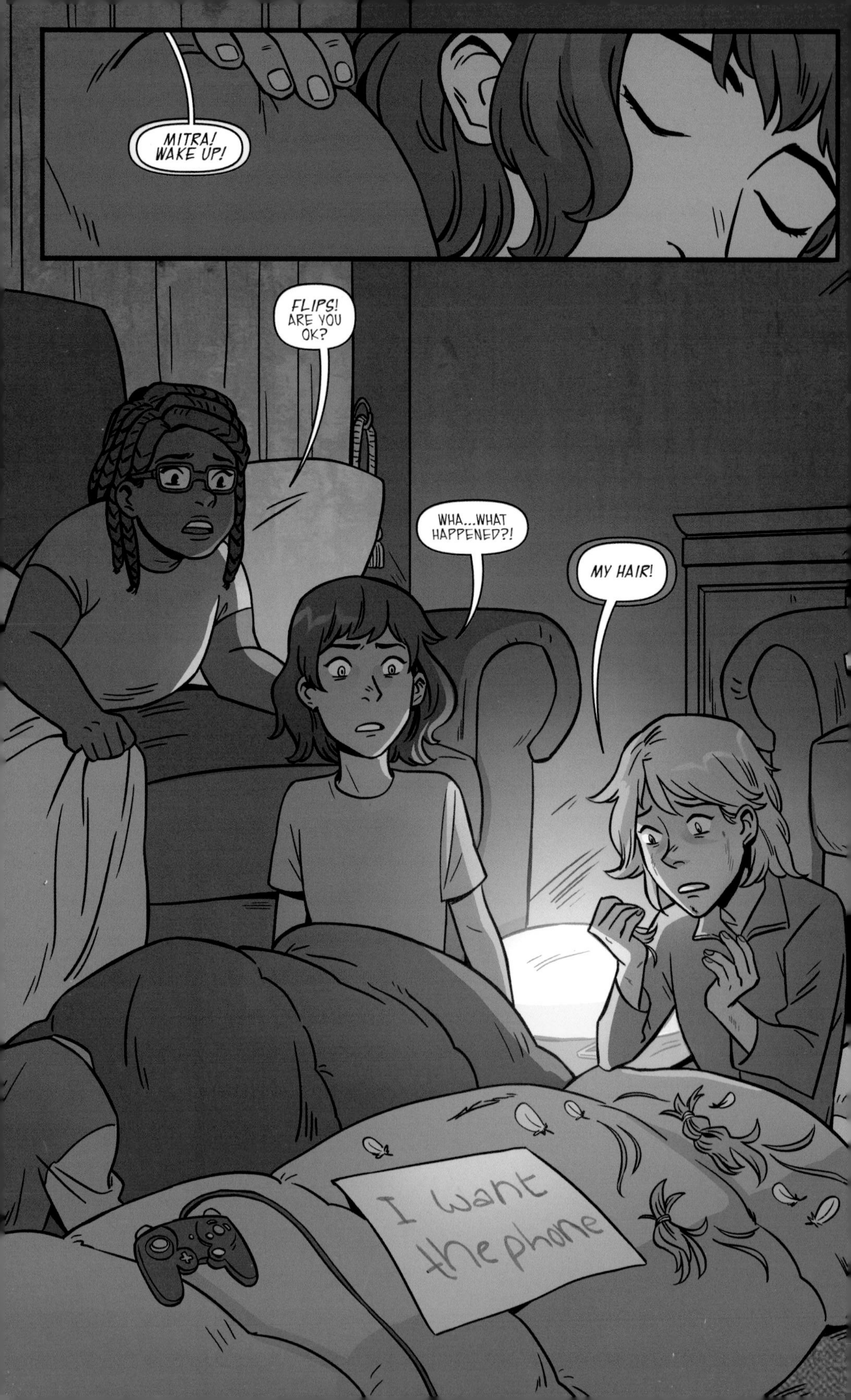
MITRA! WAKE UP!
FLIPS! ARE YOU OK?
WHA...WHAT HAPPENED?!
MY HAIR!
I want the phone

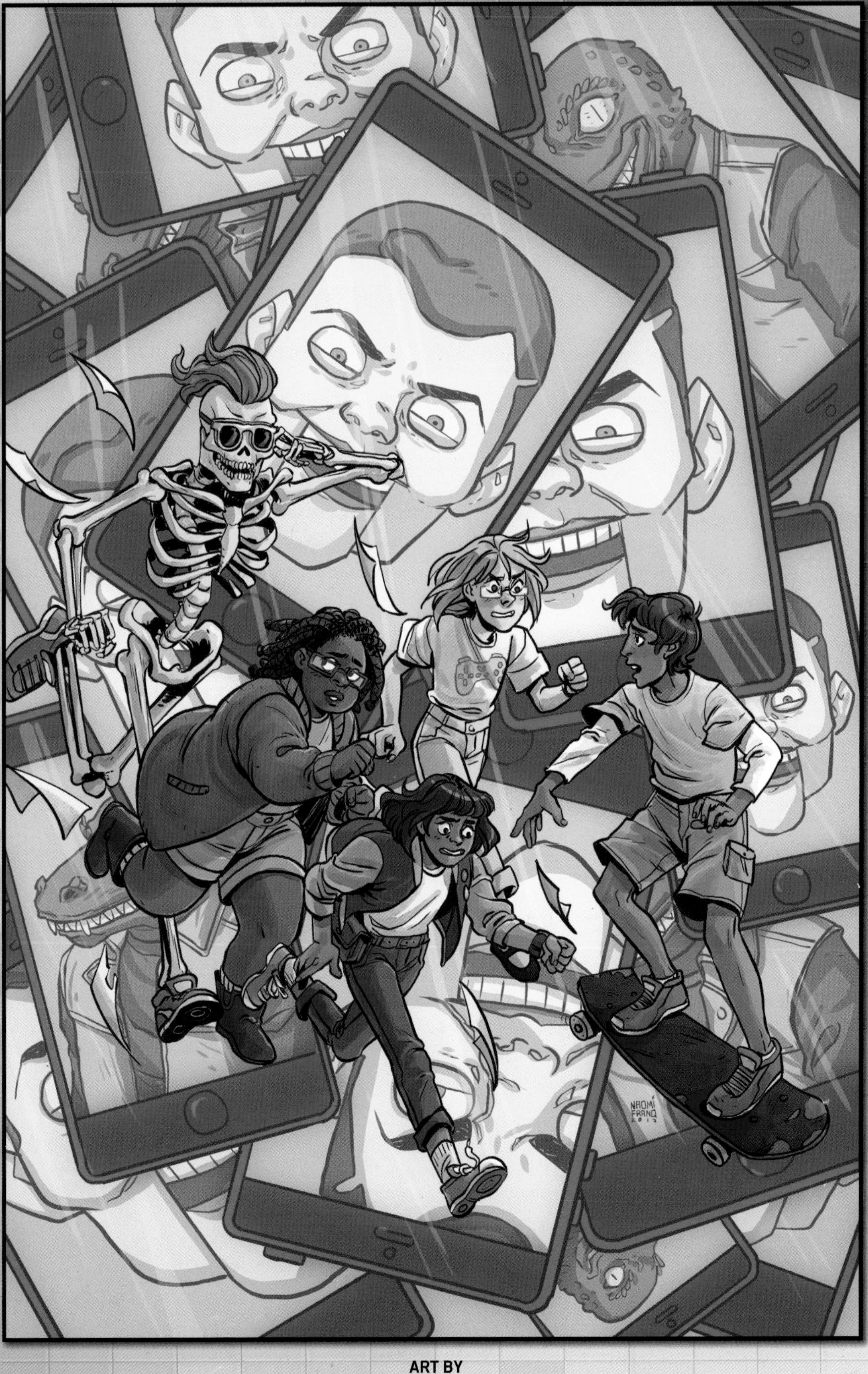
NAOMI FRANQ

ART BY
NAOMI FRANQUIZ

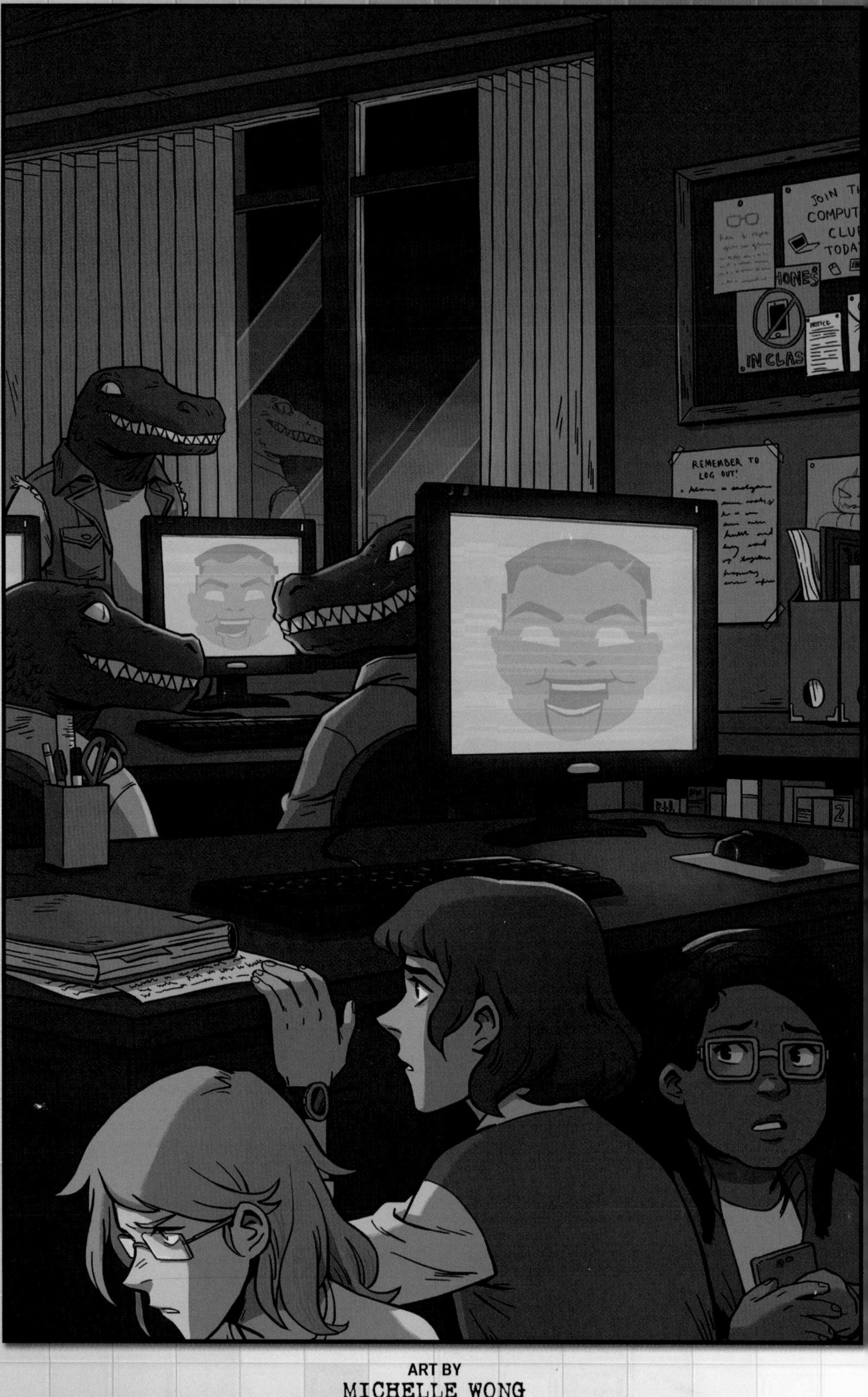
REMEMBER TO LOG OUT!

ART BY
MICHELLE WONG

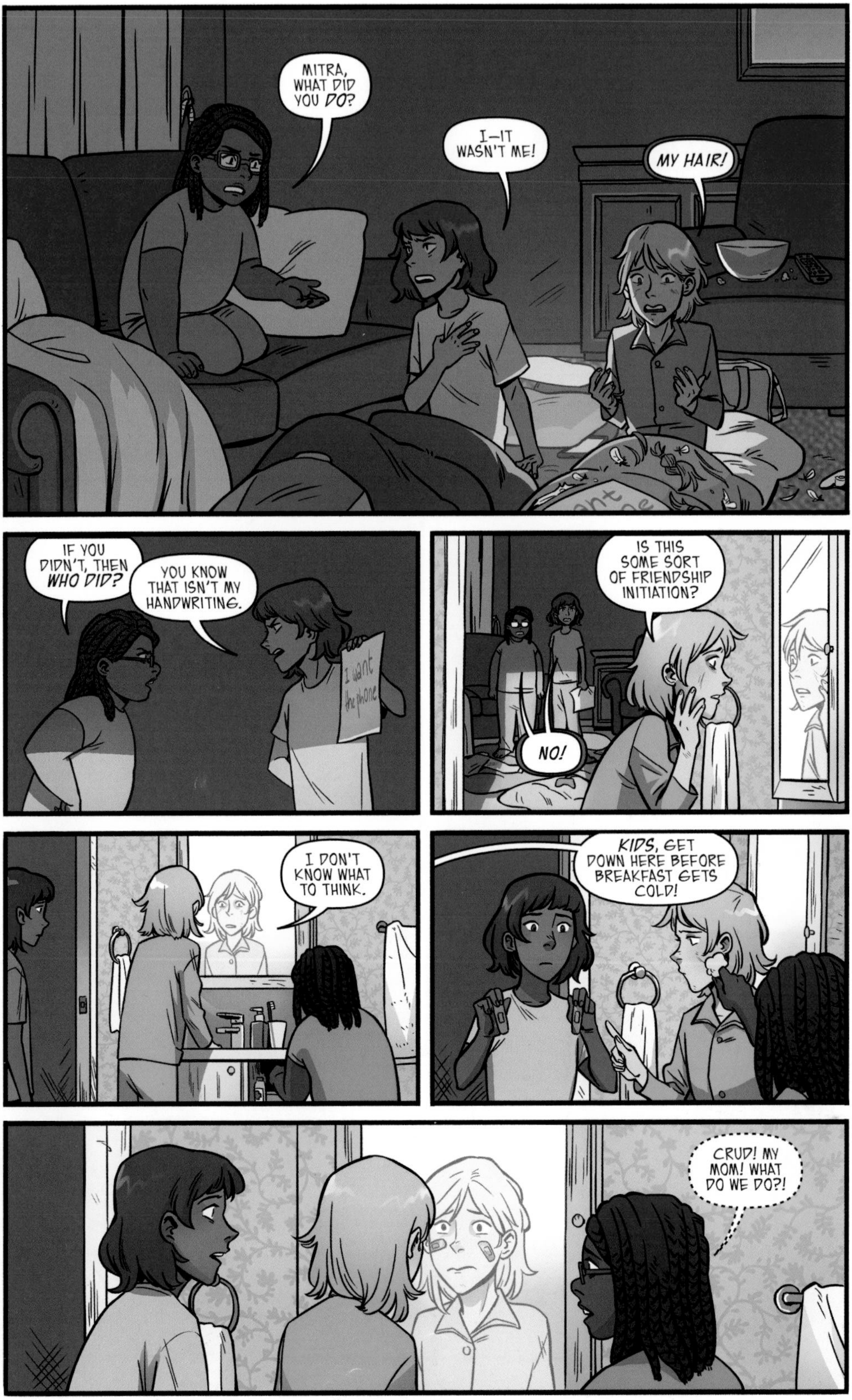
MITRA, WHAT DID YOU DO?
I—IT WASN'T ME!
MY HAIR!
IF YOU DIDN'T, THEN WHO DID?
YOU KNOW THAT ISN'T MY HANDWRITING.
I want the phone
IS THIS SOME SORT OF FRIENDSHIP INITIATION?
NO!
I DON'T KNOW WHAT TO THINK.
KIDS, GET DOWN HERE BEFORE BREAKFAST GETS COLD!
CRUD! MY MOM! WHAT DO WE DO?!

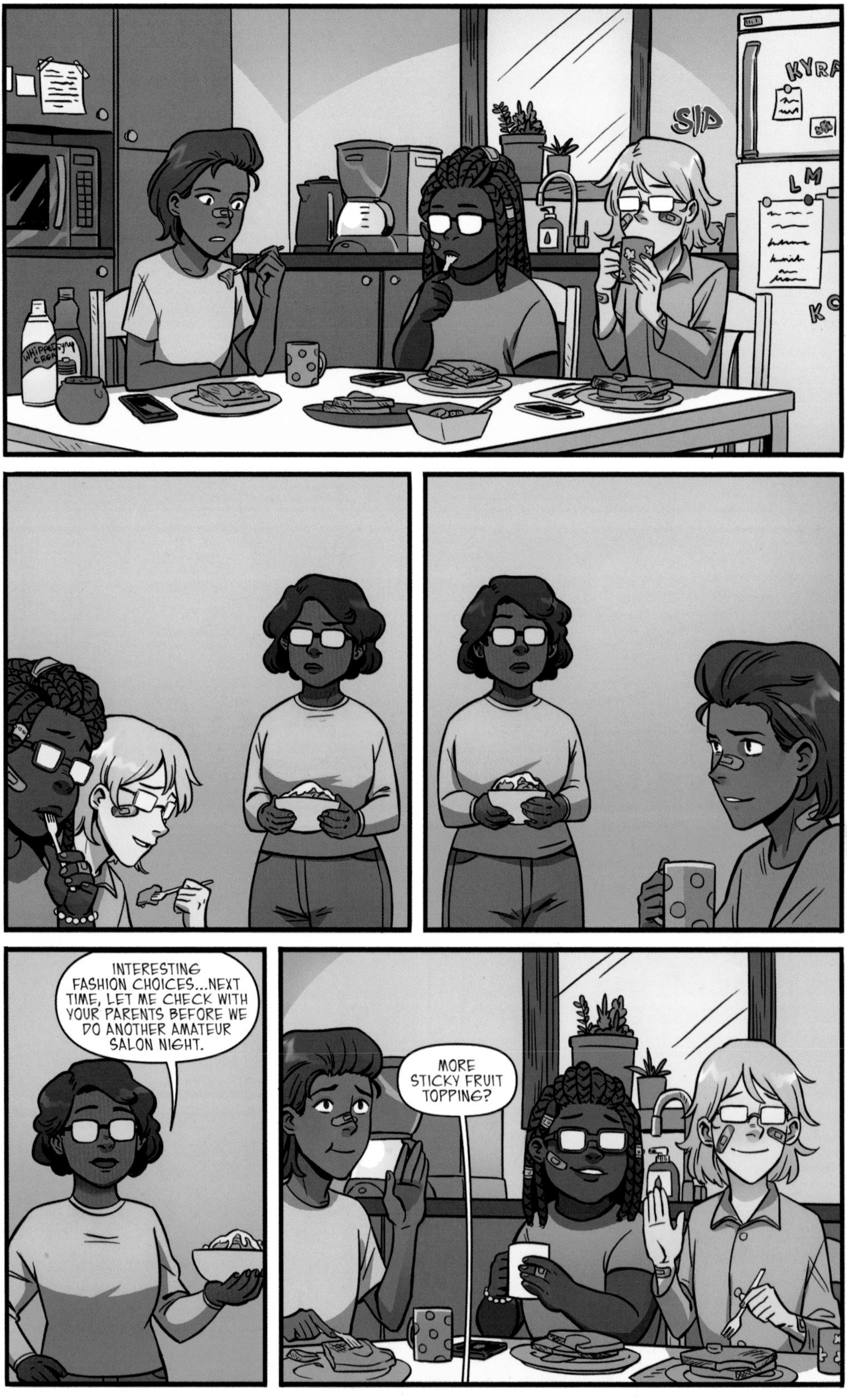
WHIPPED CREAM
SYRUP
KYRA
SIP
LM
KO
INTERESTING FASHION CHOICES...NEXT TIME, LET ME CHECK WITH YOUR PARENTS BEFORE WE DO ANOTHER AMATEUR SALON NIGHT.
MORE STICKY FRUIT TOPPING?

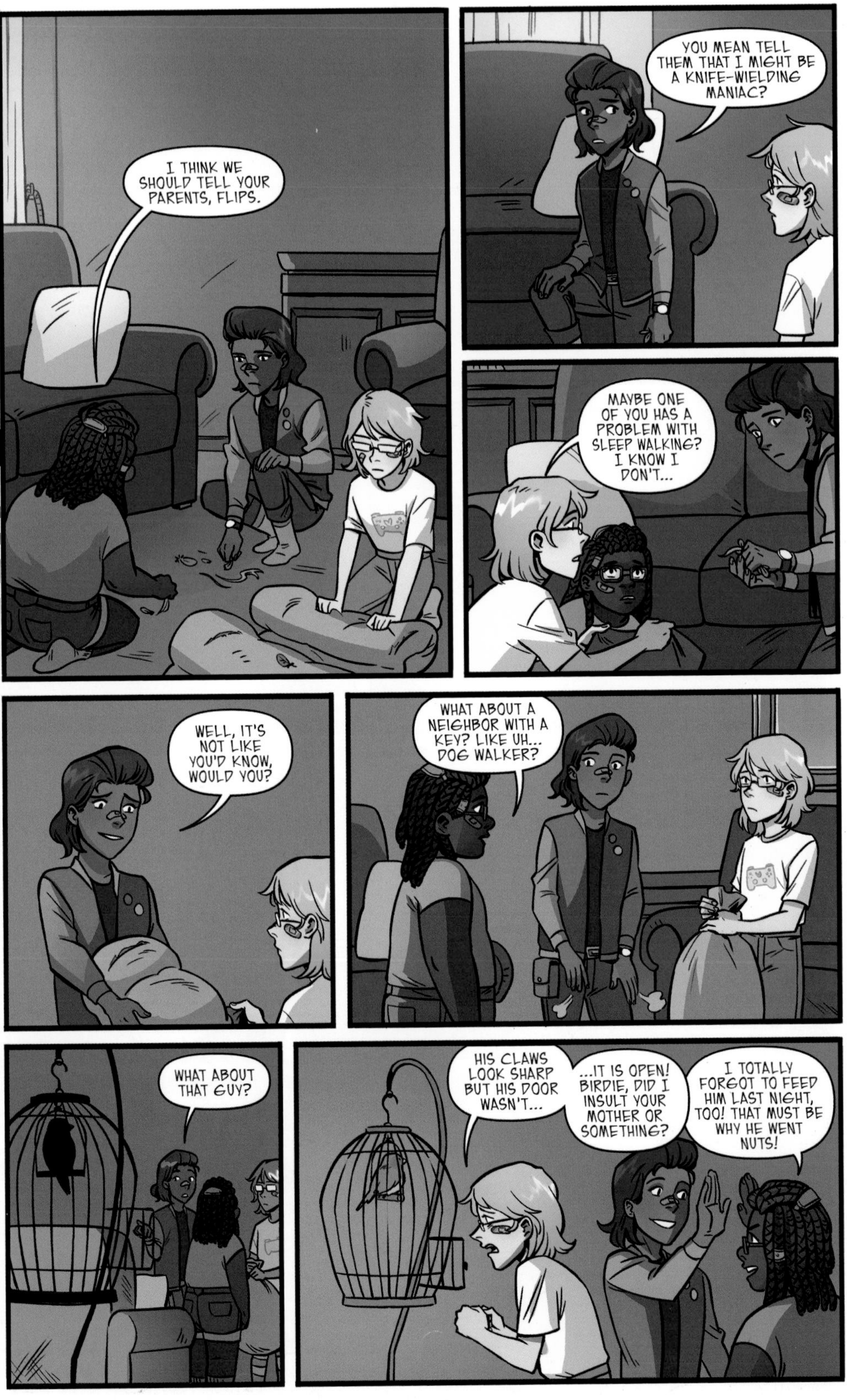
I THINK WE SHOULD TELL YOUR PARENTS, FLIPS.
YOU MEAN TELL THEM THAT I MIGHT BE A KNIFE-WIELDING MANIAC?
MAYBE ONE OF YOU HAS A PROBLEM WITH SLEEP WALKING? I KNOW I DON'T...
WELL, IT'S NOT LIKE YOU'D KNOW, WOULD YOU?
WHAT ABOUT A NEIGHBOR WITH A KEY? LIKE UH... DOG WALKER?
WHAT ABOUT THAT GUY?
HIS CLAWS LOOK SHARP BUT HIS DOOR WASN'T...
...IT IS OPEN! BIRDIE, DID I INSULT YOUR MOTHER OR SOMETHING?
I TOTALLY FORGOT TO FEED HIM LAST NIGHT, TOO! THAT MUST BE WHY HE WENT NUTS!

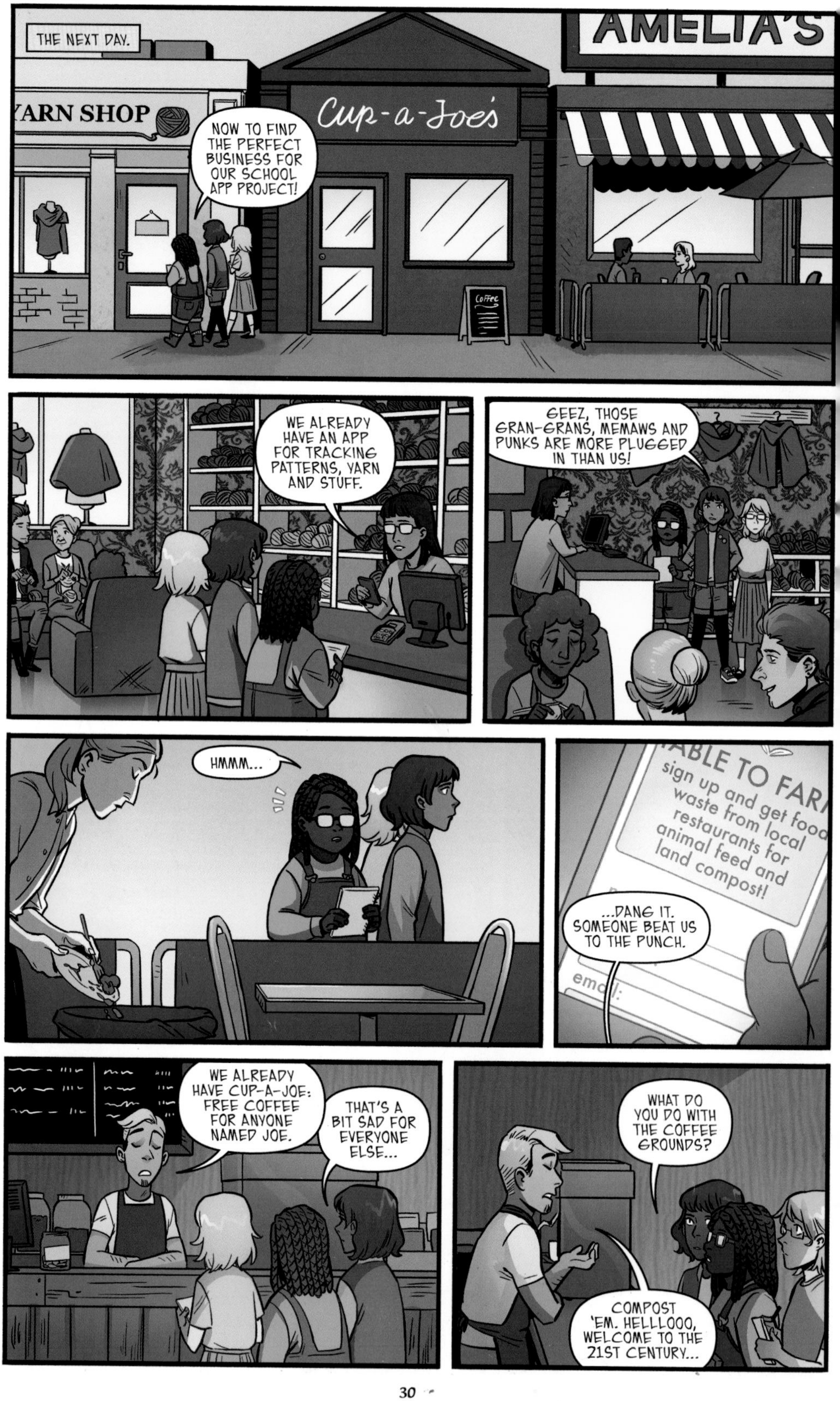
THE NEXT DAY.
AMELIA'S
YARN SHOP
Cup-a-Joe's
NOW TO FIND THE PERFECT BUSINESS FOR OUR SCHOOL APP PROJECT!
COFFEE
WE ALREADY HAVE AN APP FOR TRACKING PATTERNS, YARN AND STUFF.
GEEZ, THOSE GRAN-GRANS, MEMAWS AND PUNKS ARE MORE PLUGGED IN THAN US!
HMMM...
ABLE TO FAR
sign up and get food waste from local restaurants for animal feed and land compost!
...DANG IT. SOMEONE BEAT US TO THE PUNCH.
WE ALREADY HAVE CUP-A-JOE: FREE COFFEE FOR ANYONE NAMED JOE.
THAT'S A BIT SAD FOR EVERYONE ELSE...
WHAT DO YOU DO WITH THE COFFEE GROUNDS?
COMPOST 'EM. HELLLOOO, WELCOME TO THE 21ST CENTURY...

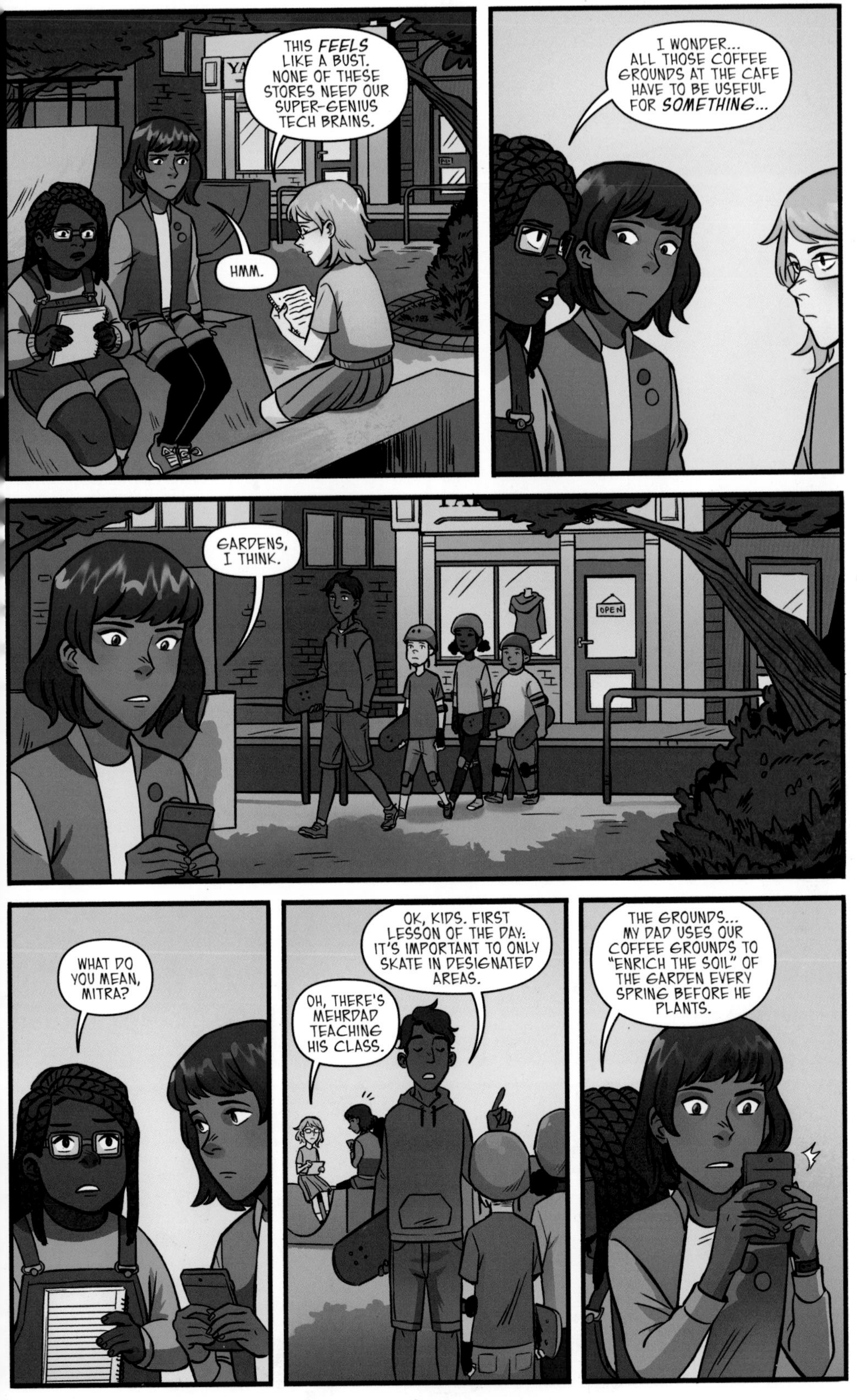
THIS FEELS LIKE A BUST. NONE OF THESE STORES NEED OUR SUPER-GENIUS TECH BRAINS.
HMM.
I WONDER... ALL THOSE COFFEE GROUNDS AT THE CAFE HAVE TO BE USEFUL FOR SOMETHING...
GARDENS, I THINK.
OPEN
WHAT DO YOU MEAN, MITRA?
OK, KIDS. FIRST LESSON OF THE DAY: IT'S IMPORTANT TO ONLY SKATE IN DESIGNATED AREAS.
OH, THERE'S MEHRDAD TEACHING HIS CLASS.
THE GROUNDS... MY DAD USES OUR COFFEE GROUNDS TO "ENRICH THE SOIL" OF THE GARDEN EVERY SPRING BEFORE HE PLANTS.

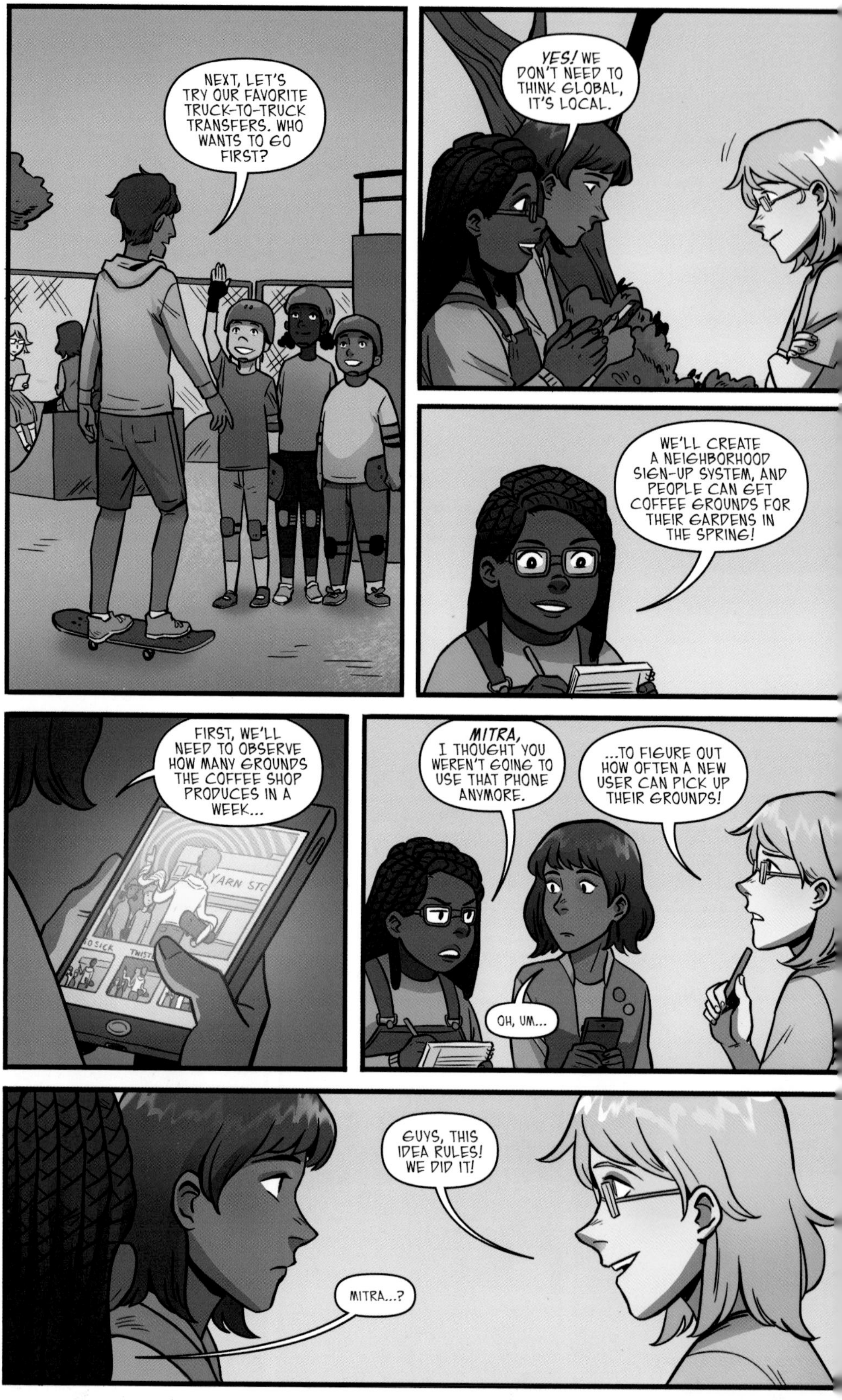
NEXT, LET'S TRY OUR FAVORITE TRUCK-TO-TRUCK TRANSFERS. WHO WANTS TO GO FIRST?
YES! WE DON'T NEED TO THINK GLOBAL, IT'S LOCAL.
WE'LL CREATE A NEIGHBORHOOD SIGN-UP SYSTEM, AND PEOPLE CAN GET COFFEE GROUNDS FOR THEIR GARDENS IN THE SPRING!
FIRST, WE'LL NEED TO OBSERVE HOW MANY GROUNDS THE COFFEE SHOP PRODUCES IN A WEEK...
YARN STO
MITRA, I THOUGHT YOU WEREN'T GOING TO USE THAT PHONE ANYMORE.
...TO FIGURE OUT HOW OFTEN A NEW USER CAN PICK UP THEIR GROUNDS!
OH, UM...
GUYS, THIS IDEA RULES! WE DID IT!
MITRA...?

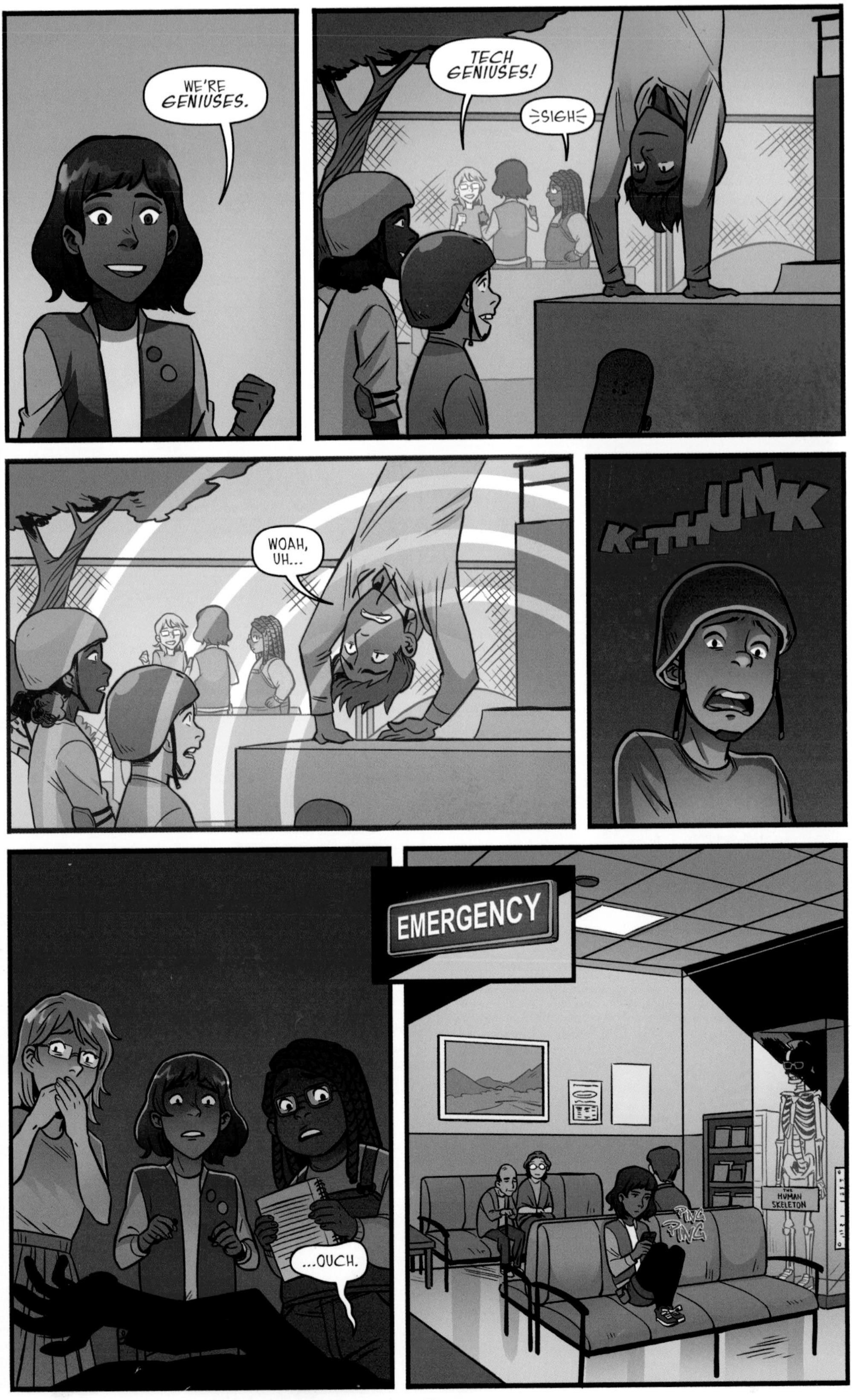
WE'RE GENIUSES.
TECH GENIUSES!
SIGH
WOAH, UH...
K-THUNK
...OUCH.
EMERGENCY
PING PING
THE HUMAN SKELETON

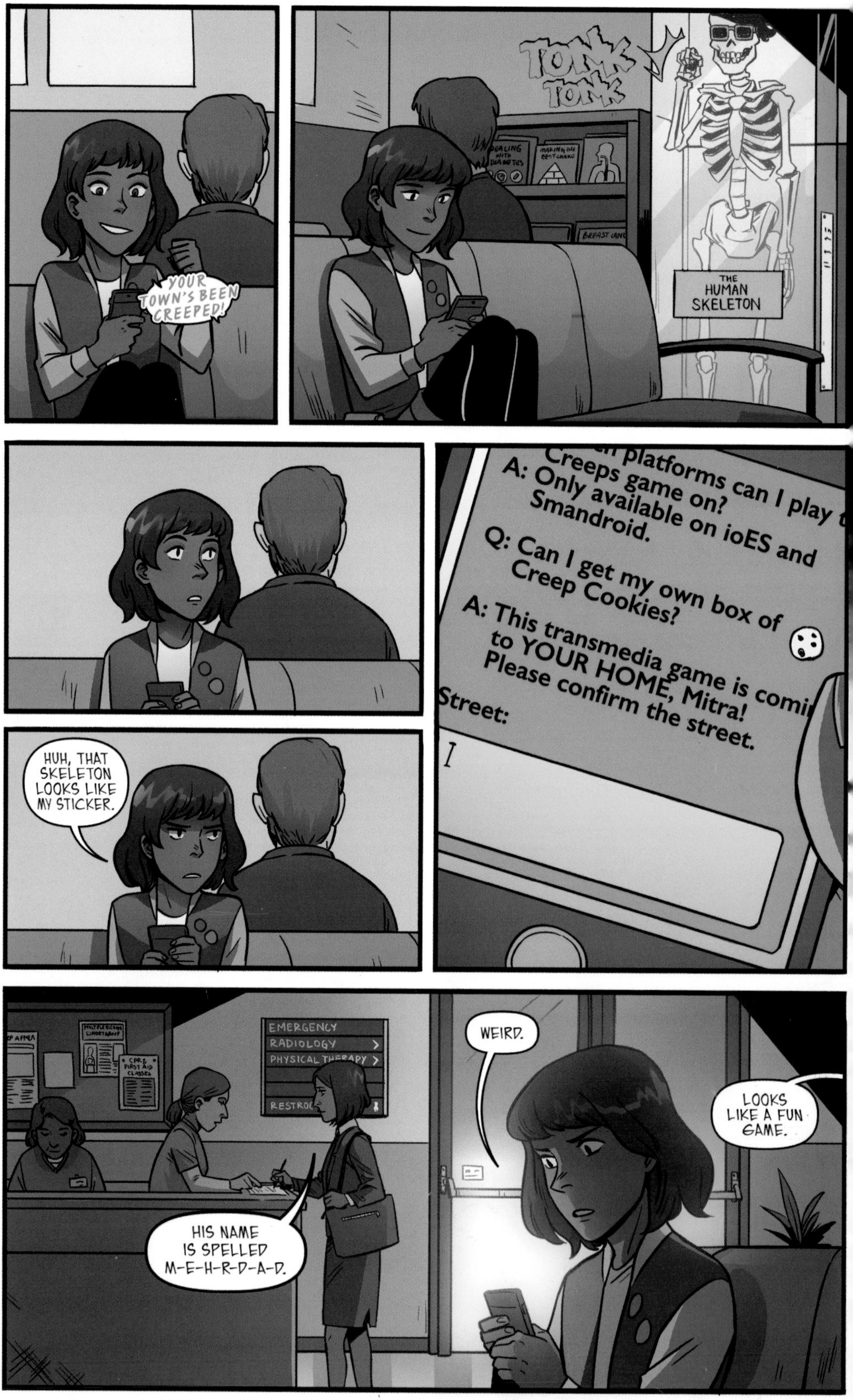
YOUR TOWN'S BEEN CREEPED!
TONK TONK
DEALING WITH DIABETES
MAKING THE BEST CHOICE
BREAST CAN
THE HUMAN SKELETON
platforms can I play t
Creeps game on?
A: Only available on ioES and Smandroid.
Q: Can I get my own box of Creep Cookies?
A: This transmedia game is comi
to YOUR HOME, Mitra!
Please confirm the street.
Street:
HUH, THAT SKELETON LOOKS LIKE MY STICKER.
EMERGENCY
RADIOLOGY
PHYSICAL THERAPY
RESTRO
CPR & FIRST AID CLASSES
WEIRD.
LOOKS LIKE A FUN GAME.
HIS NAME IS SPELLED M-E-H-R-D-A-D.

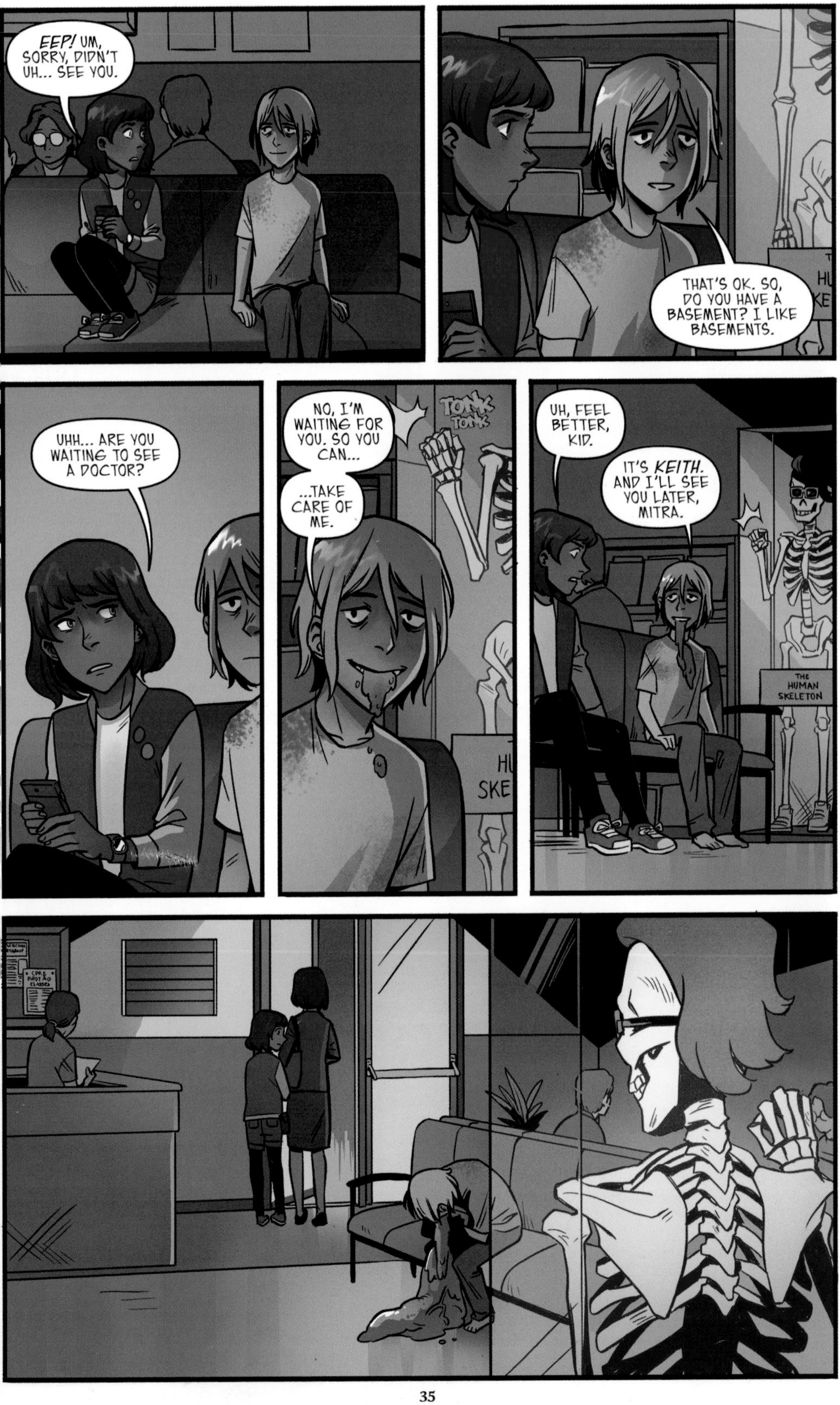
EEP! UM, SORRY, DIDN'T UH... SEE YOU.
THAT'S OK. SO, DO YOU HAVE A BASEMENT? I LIKE BASEMENTS.
THE HUMAN SKELETON
UHH... ARE YOU WAITING TO SEE A DOCTOR?
NO, I'M WAITING FOR YOU. SO YOU CAN...
...TAKE CARE OF ME.
TONK TONK
UH, FEEL BETTER, KID.
IT'S KEITH. AND I'LL SEE YOU LATER, MITRA.
THE HUMAN SKELETON
CPR & FIRST AID CLASSES

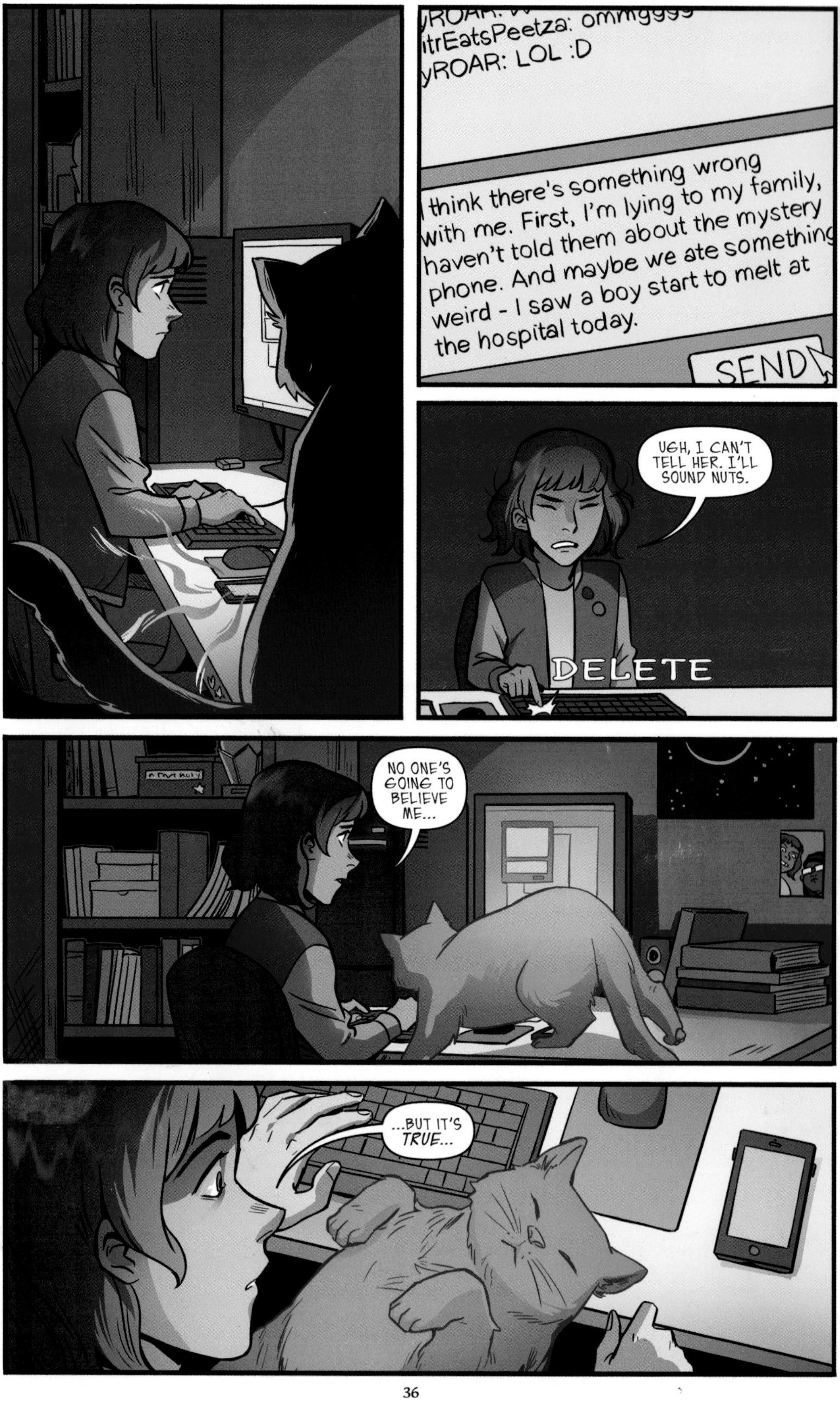
yROAR: W
itrEatsPeetza: ommgggg
yROAR: LOL :D
I think there's something wrong with me. First, I'm lying to my family, haven't told them about the mystery phone. And maybe we ate something weird - I saw a boy start to melt at the hospital today.
SEND
UGH, I CAN'T TELL HER. I'LL SOUND NUTS.
DELETE
NO ONE'S GOING TO BELIEVE ME...
...BUT IT'S TRUE...

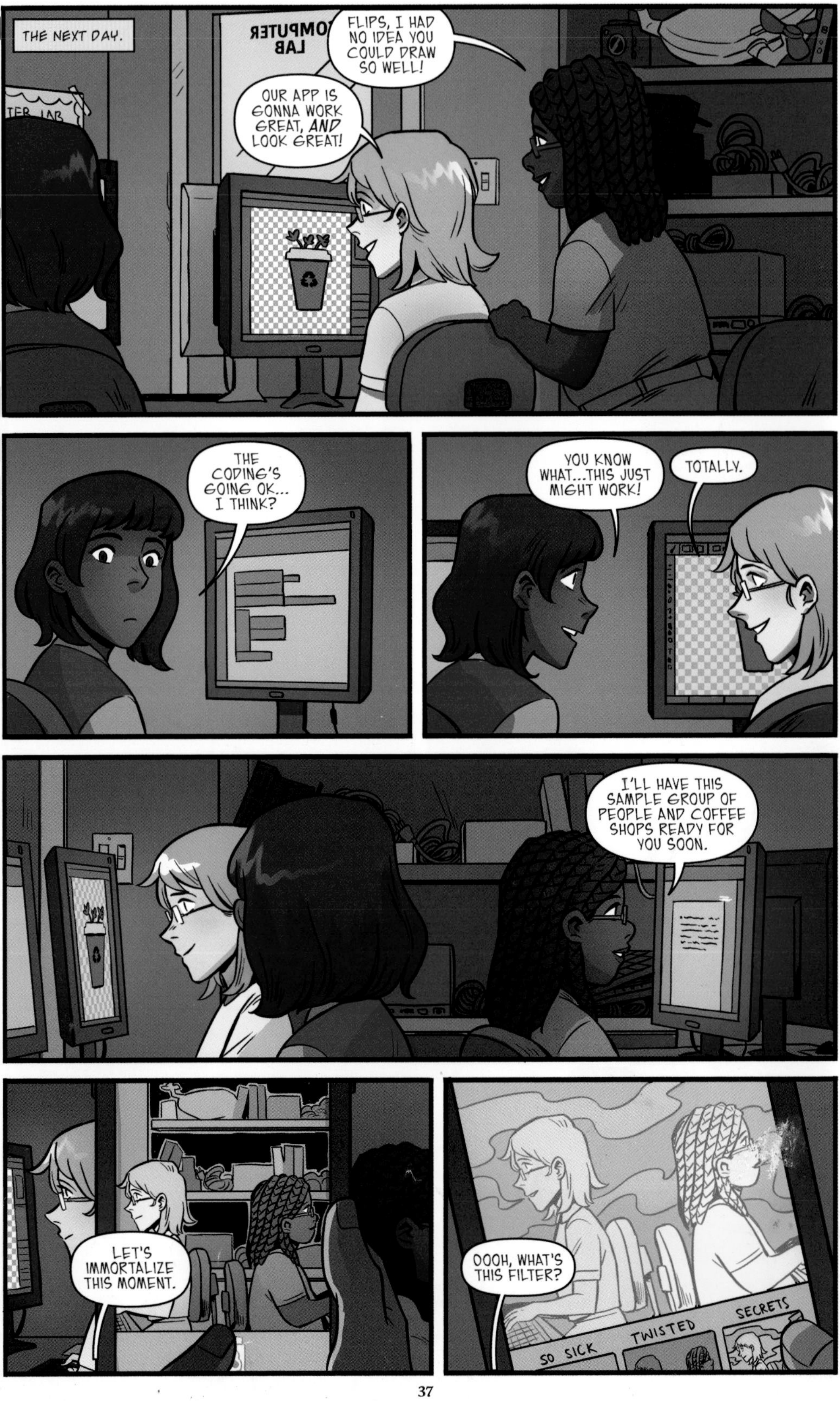
THE NEXT DAY.
FLIPS, I HAD NO IDEA YOU COULD DRAW SO WELL!
OUR APP IS GONNA WORK GREAT, AND LOOK GREAT!
THE CODING'S GOING OK... I THINK?
YOU KNOW WHAT...THIS JUST MIGHT WORK!
TOTALLY.
I'LL HAVE THIS SAMPLE GROUP OF PEOPLE AND COFFEE SHOPS READY FOR YOU SOON.
LET'S IMMORTALIZE THIS MOMENT.
OOOH, WHAT'S THIS FILTER?
SO SICK
TWISTED
SECRETS

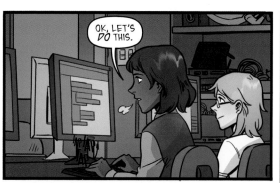

OK, LET'S DO THIS.
set FAMILY to 1
repeat while FAMILY ≤
"GROUND TIME"
WHAT...IS THIS A BUG?
I JUST WANT TO HANG OUT WITH YOU.
KNOCK KNOCK!
THINK YOUR TEAM COULD GIVE YOU A BREAK, MITRA?
W..WEATHER!

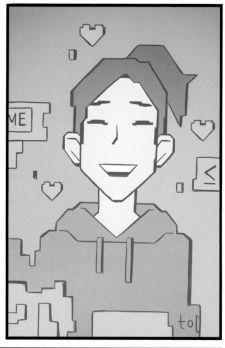

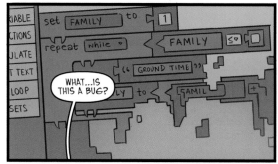

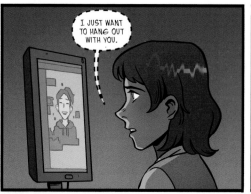

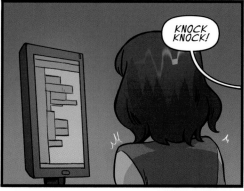

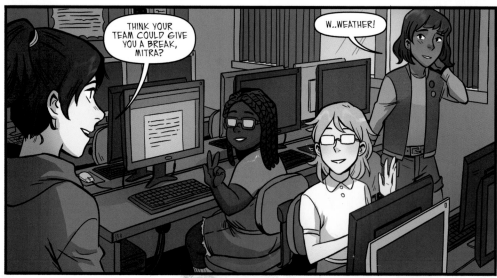

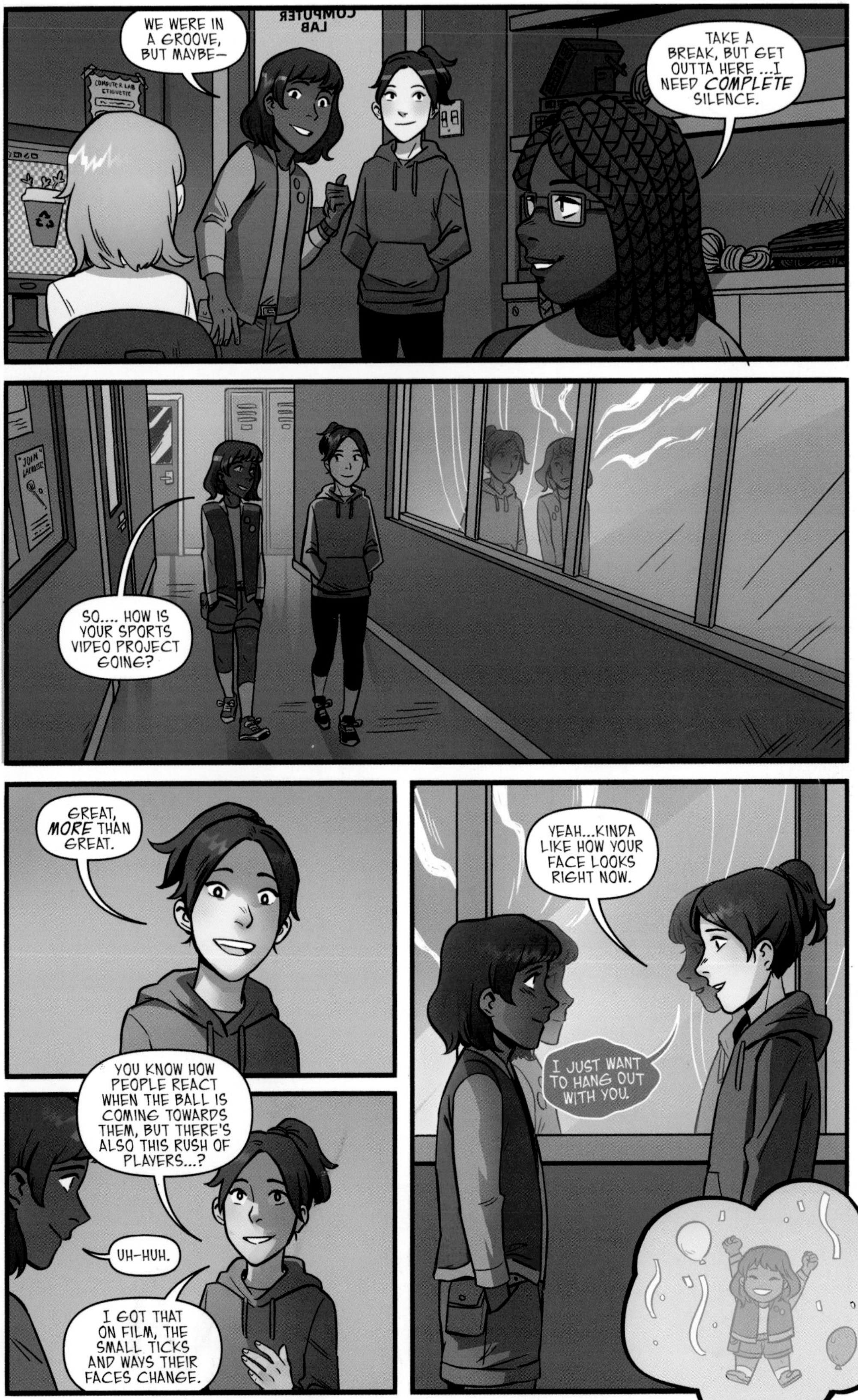
COMPUTER LAB
COMPUTER LAB ETIQUETTE
WE WERE IN A GROOVE, BUT MAYBE—
TAKE A BREAK, BUT GET OUTTA HERE ...I NEED COMPLETE SILENCE.
"JOIN LACROSSE"
SO.... HOW IS YOUR SPORTS VIDEO PROJECT GOING?
GREAT, MORE THAN GREAT.
YOU KNOW HOW PEOPLE REACT WHEN THE BALL IS COMING TOWARDS THEM, BUT THERE'S ALSO THIS RUSH OF PLAYERS...?
UH-HUH.
I GOT THAT ON FILM, THE SMALL TICKS AND WAYS THEIR FACES CHANGE.
YEAH...KINDA LIKE HOW YOUR FACE LOOKS RIGHT NOW.
I JUST WANT TO HANG OUT WITH YOU.

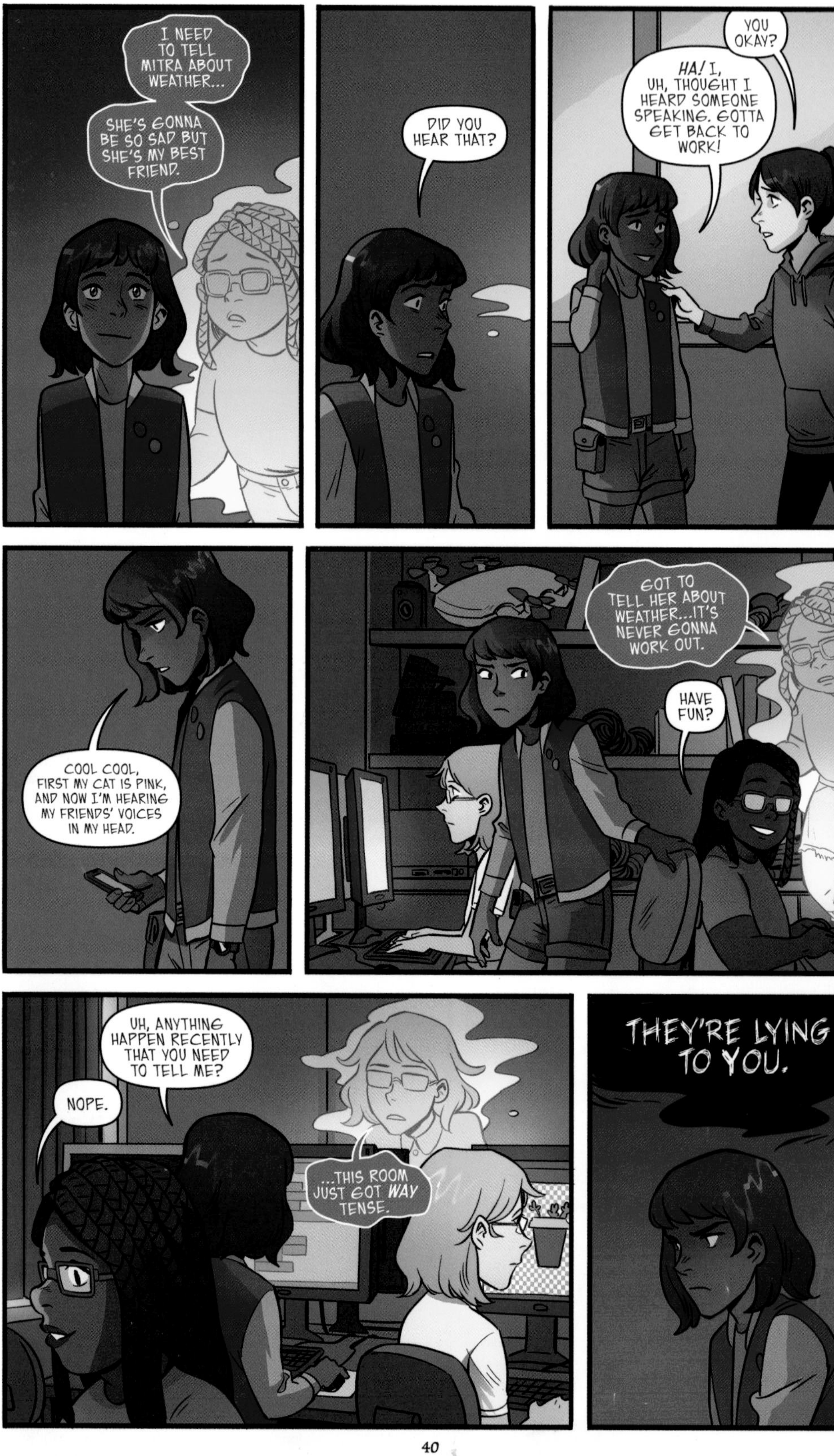
I NEED TO TELL MITRA ABOUT WEATHER...
SHE'S GONNA BE SO SAD BUT SHE'S MY BEST FRIEND.
DID YOU HEAR THAT?
YOU OKAY?
HA! I, UH, THOUGHT I HEARD SOMEONE SPEAKING. GOTTA GET BACK TO WORK!
COOL COOL, FIRST MY CAT IS PINK, AND NOW I'M HEARING MY FRIENDS' VOICES IN MY HEAD.
GOT TO TELL HER ABOUT WEATHER...IT'S NEVER GONNA WORK OUT.
HAVE FUN?
UH, ANYTHING HAPPEN RECENTLY THAT YOU NEED TO TELL ME?
NOPE.
...THIS ROOM JUST GOT WAY TENSE.
THEY'RE LYING TO YOU.

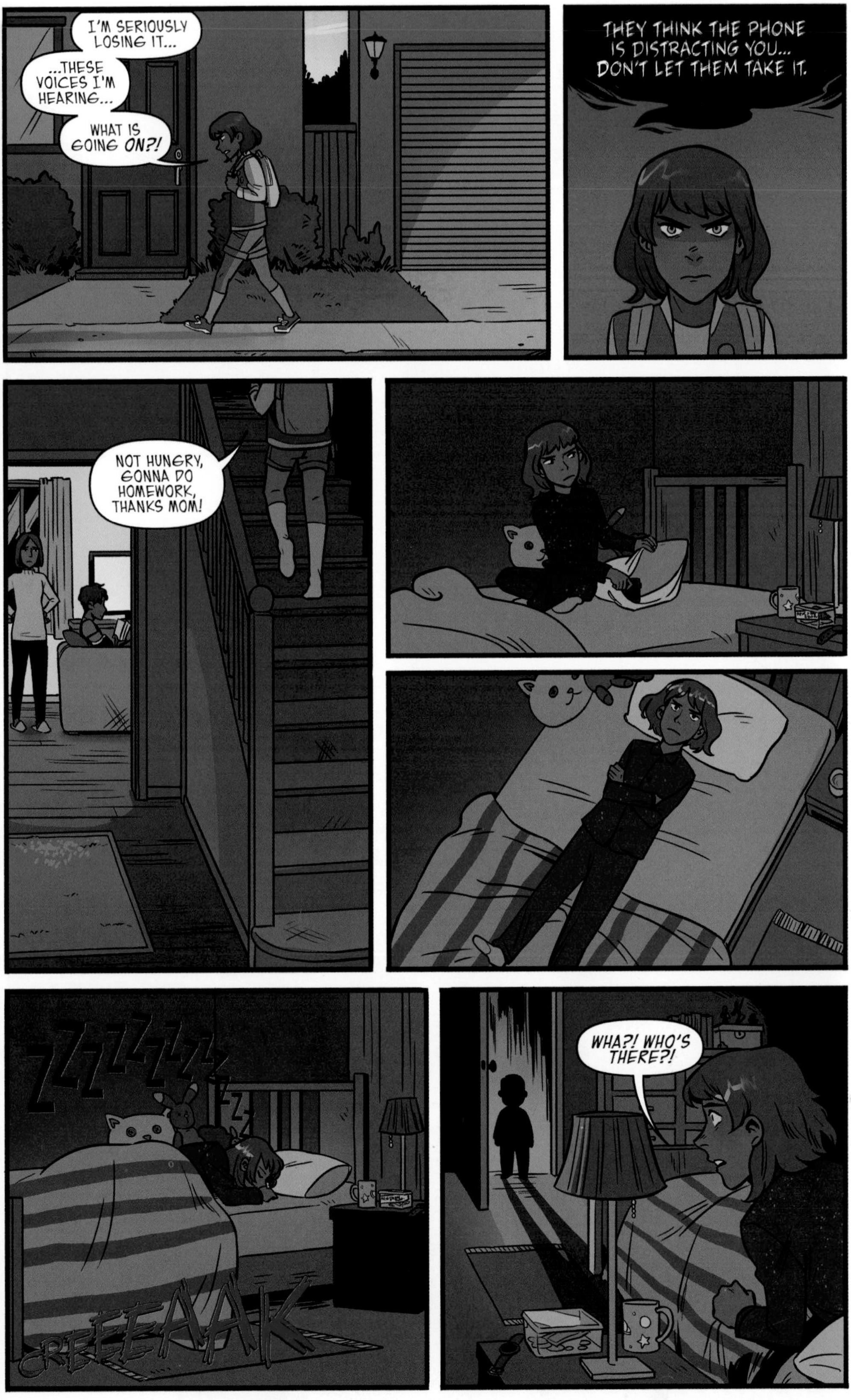
I'M SERIOUSLY LOSING IT...
...THESE VOICES I'M HEARING...
WHAT IS GOING ON?!
THEY THINK THE PHONE IS DISTRACTING YOU... DON'T LET THEM TAKE IT.
NOT HUNGRY, GONNA DO HOMEWORK, THANKS MOM!
ZZZZZZZZZ
CREEEEAAK
WHA?! WHO'S THERE?!

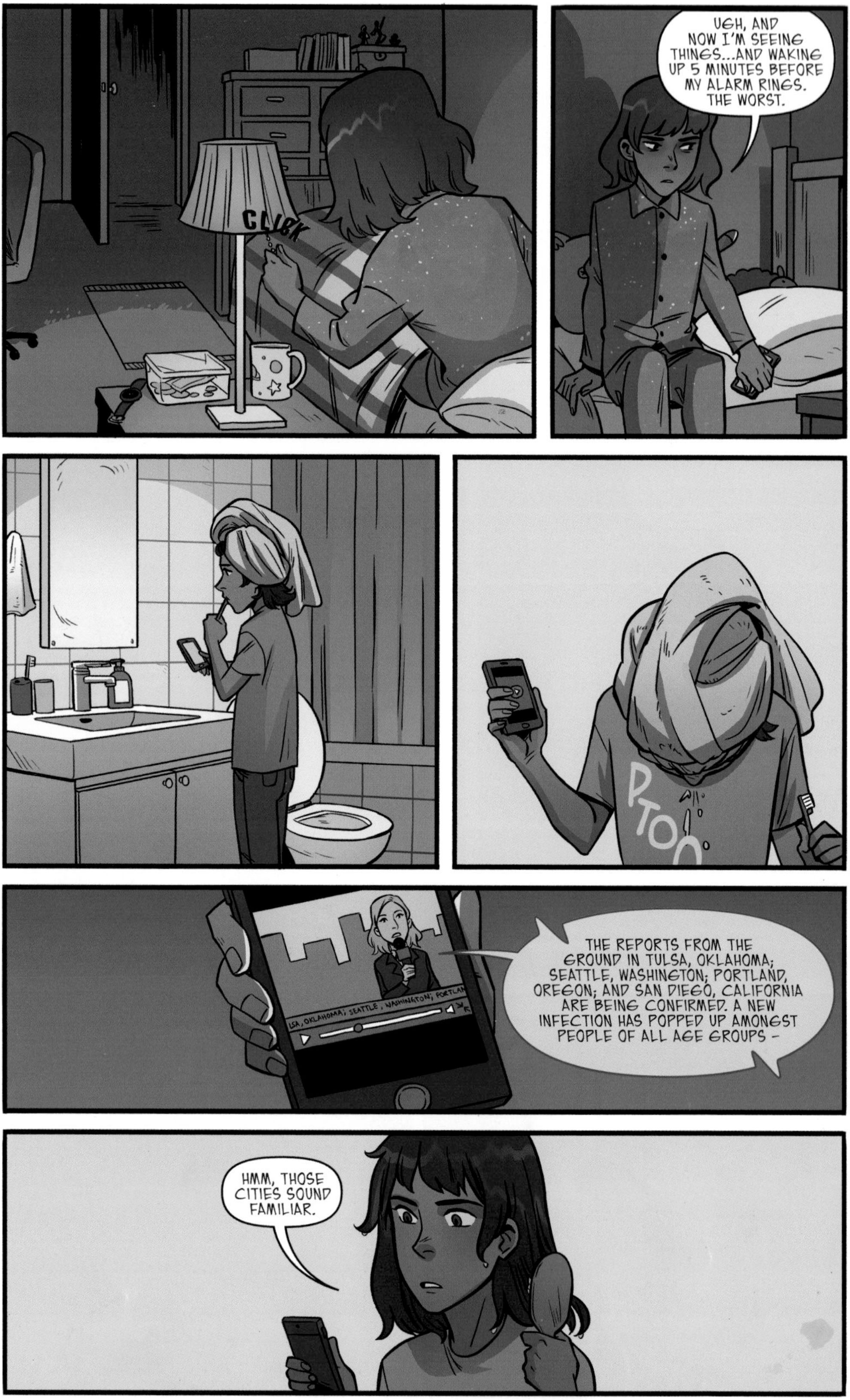
CLICK
UGH, AND NOW I'M SEEING THINGS...AND WAKING UP 5 MINUTES BEFORE MY ALARM RINGS. THE WORST.
THE REPORTS FROM THE GROUND IN TULSA, OKLAHOMA; SEATTLE, WASHINGTON; PORTLAND, OREGON; AND SAN DIEGO, CALIFORNIA ARE BEING CONFIRMED. A NEW INFECTION HAS POPPED UP AMONGST PEOPLE OF ALL AGE GROUPS –
HMM, THOSE CITIES SOUND FAMILIAR.

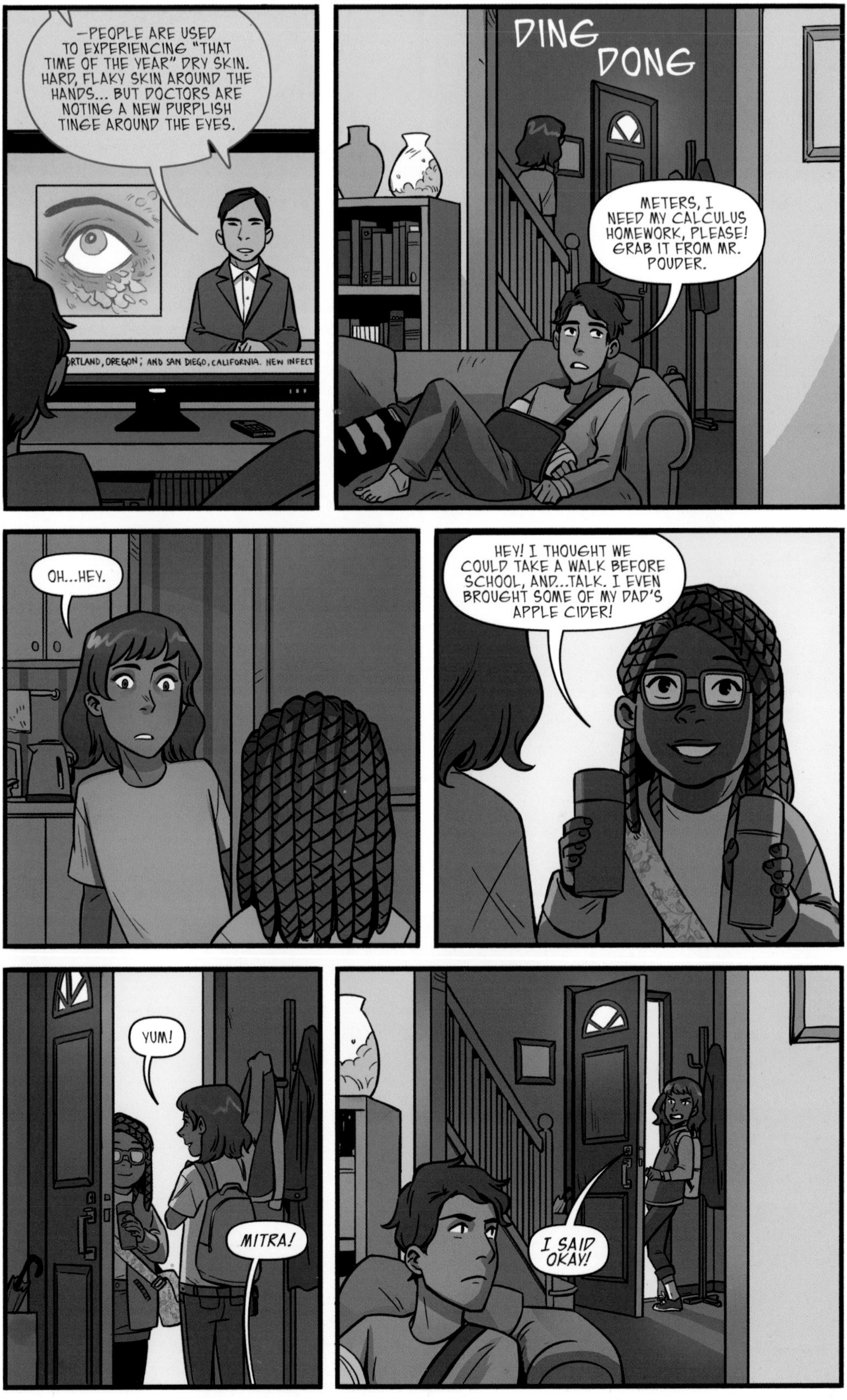
—PEOPLE ARE USED TO EXPERIENCING "THAT TIME OF THE YEAR" DRY SKIN. HARD, FLAKY SKIN AROUND THE HANDS... BUT DOCTORS ARE NOTING A NEW PURPLISH TINGE AROUND THE EYES.
RTLAND, OREGON; AND SAN DIEGO, CALIFORNIA. NEW INFECT
DING DONG
METERS, I NEED MY CALCULUS HOMEWORK, PLEASE! GRAB IT FROM MR. POUDER.
OH...HEY.
HEY! I THOUGHT WE COULD TAKE A WALK BEFORE SCHOOL, AND...TALK. I EVEN BROUGHT SOME OF MY DAD'S APPLE CIDER!
YUM!
MITRA!
I SAID OKAY!

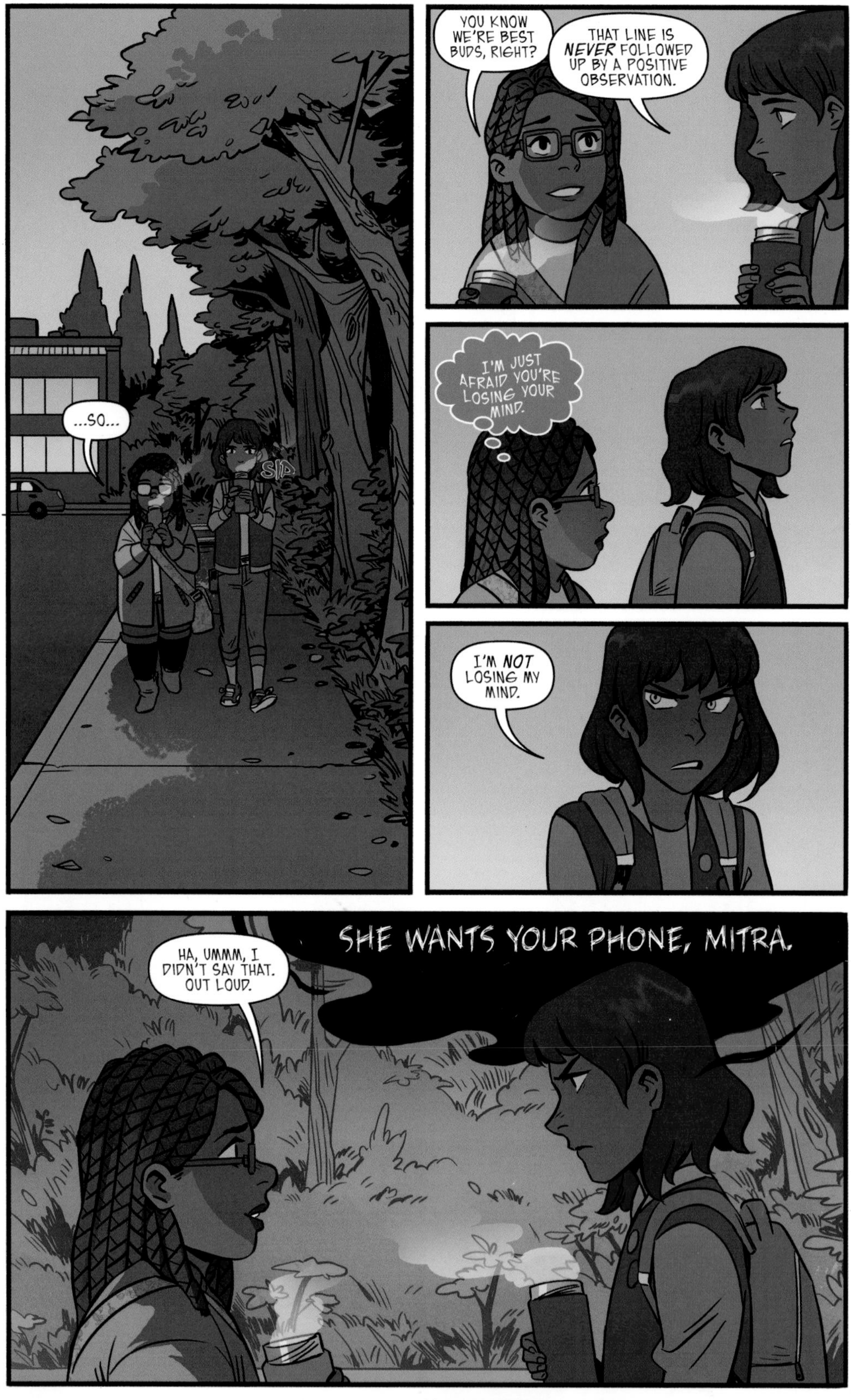
...SO...
SIP
YOU KNOW WE'RE BEST BUDS, RIGHT?
THAT LINE IS NEVER FOLLOWED UP BY A POSITIVE OBSERVATION.
I'M JUST AFRAID YOU'RE LOSING YOUR MIND.
I'M NOT LOSING MY MIND.
HA, UMMM, I DIDN'T SAY THAT. OUT LOUD.
SHE WANTS YOUR PHONE, MITRA.

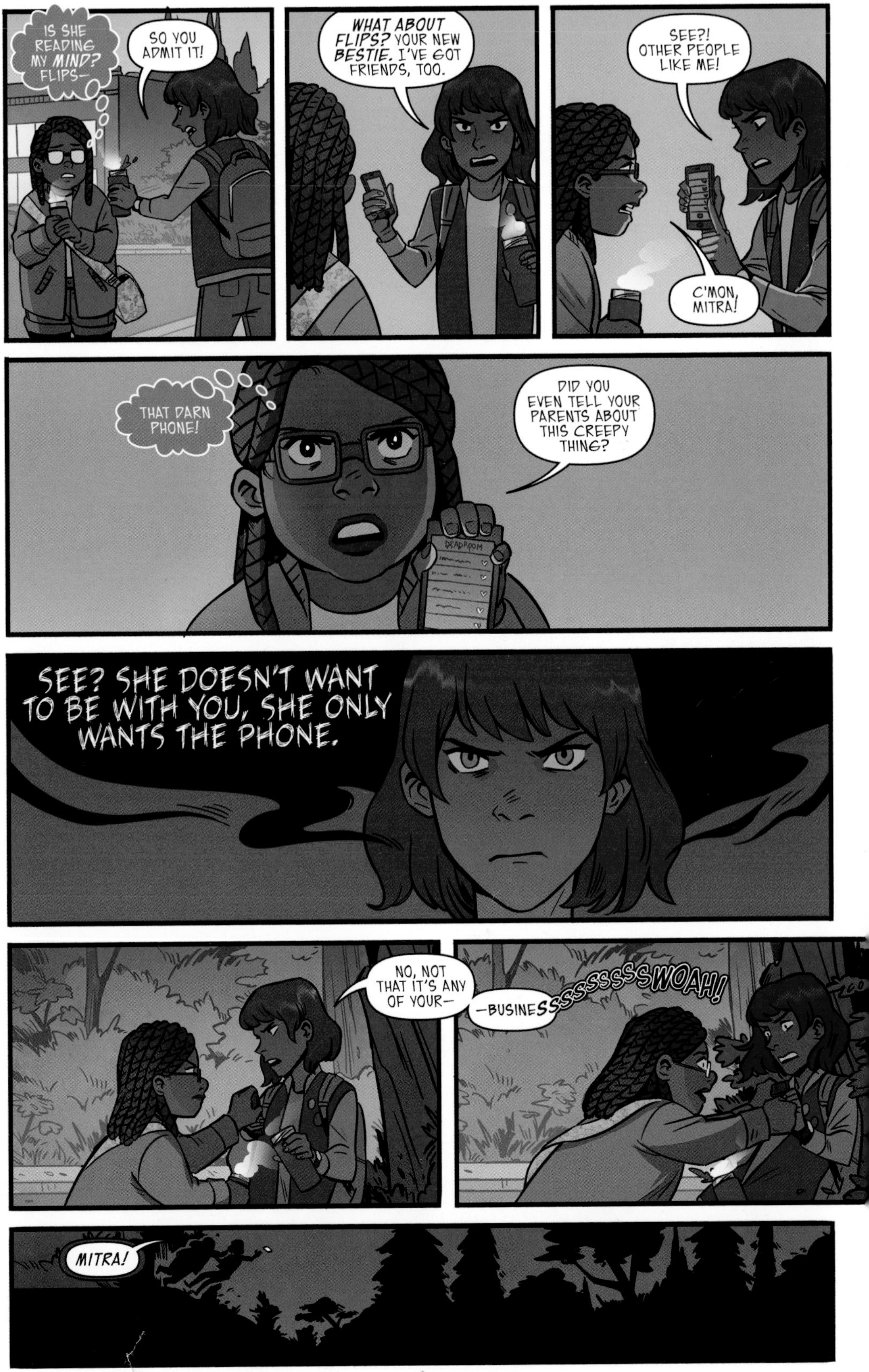
IS SHE READING MY MIND? FLIPS—
SO YOU ADMIT IT!
WHAT ABOUT FLIPS? YOUR NEW BESTIE. I'VE GOT FRIENDS, TOO.
SEE?! OTHER PEOPLE LIKE ME!
C'MON, MITRA!
THAT DARN PHONE!
DID YOU EVEN TELL YOUR PARENTS ABOUT THIS CREEPY THING?
DEADROOM
SEE? SHE DOESN'T WANT TO BE WITH YOU, SHE ONLY WANTS THE PHONE.
NO, NOT THAT IT'S ANY OF YOUR—
—BUSINESSSSSSSSSWOAH!
MITRA!

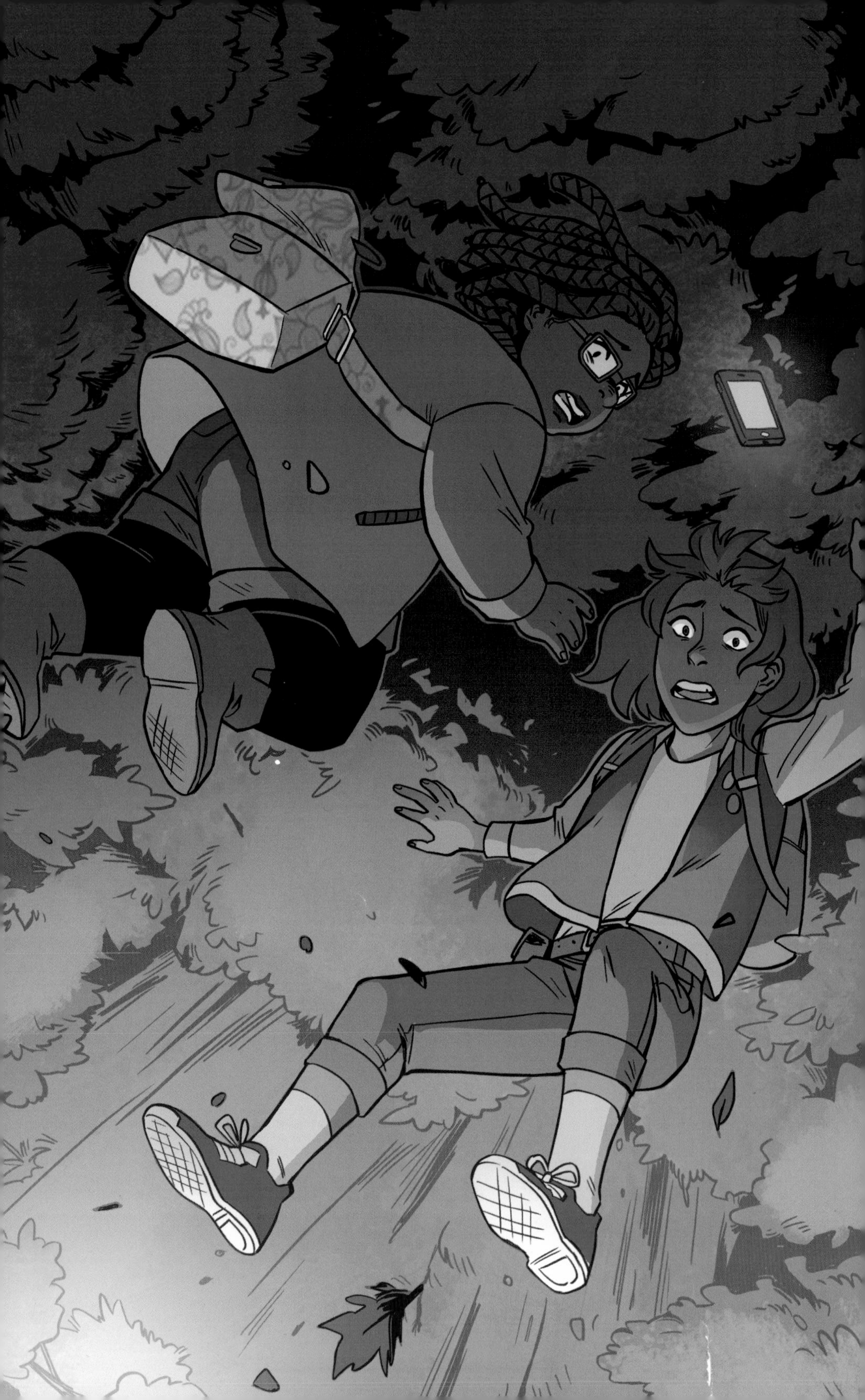

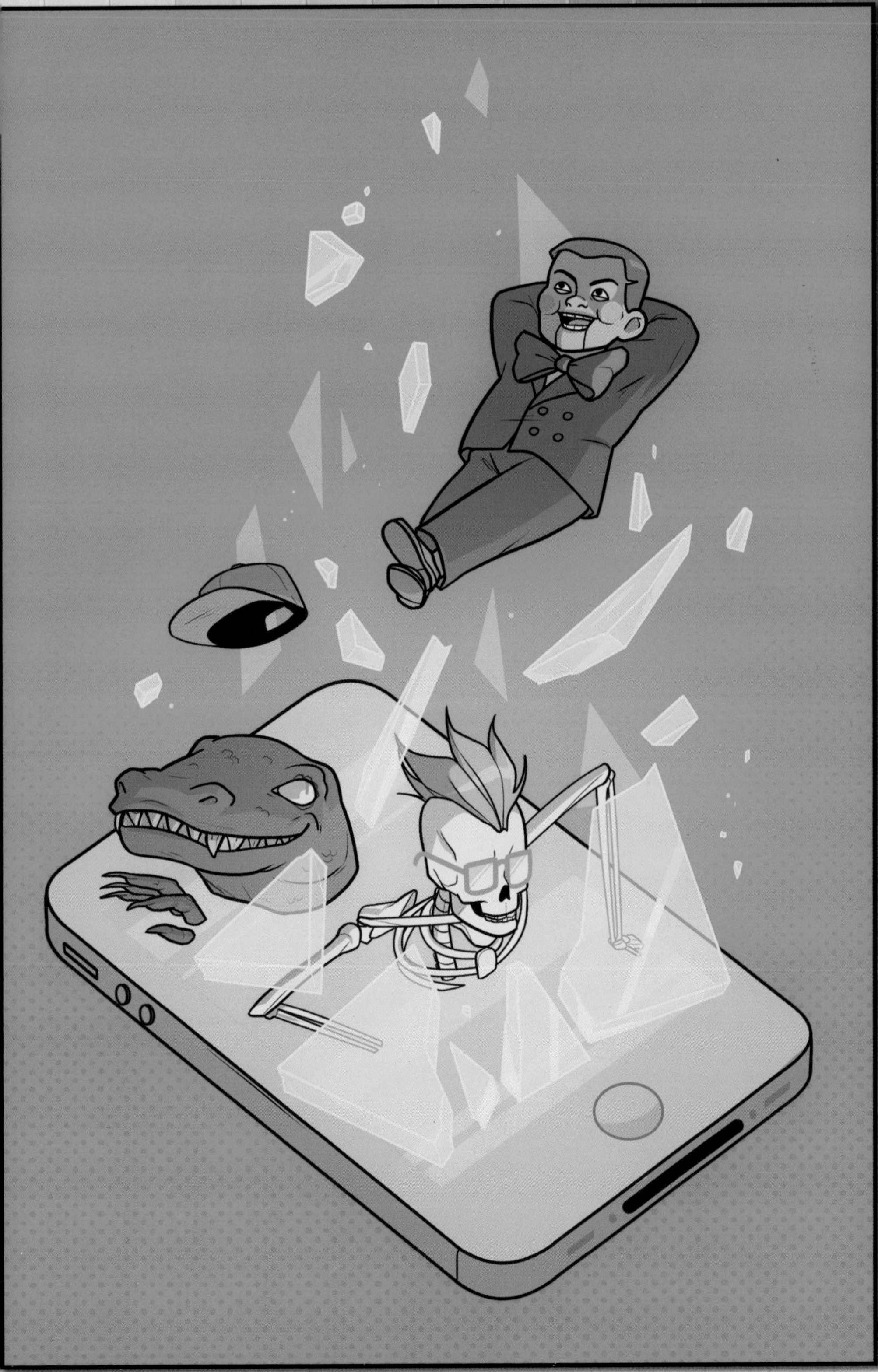

ART BY
SARA DuVALL

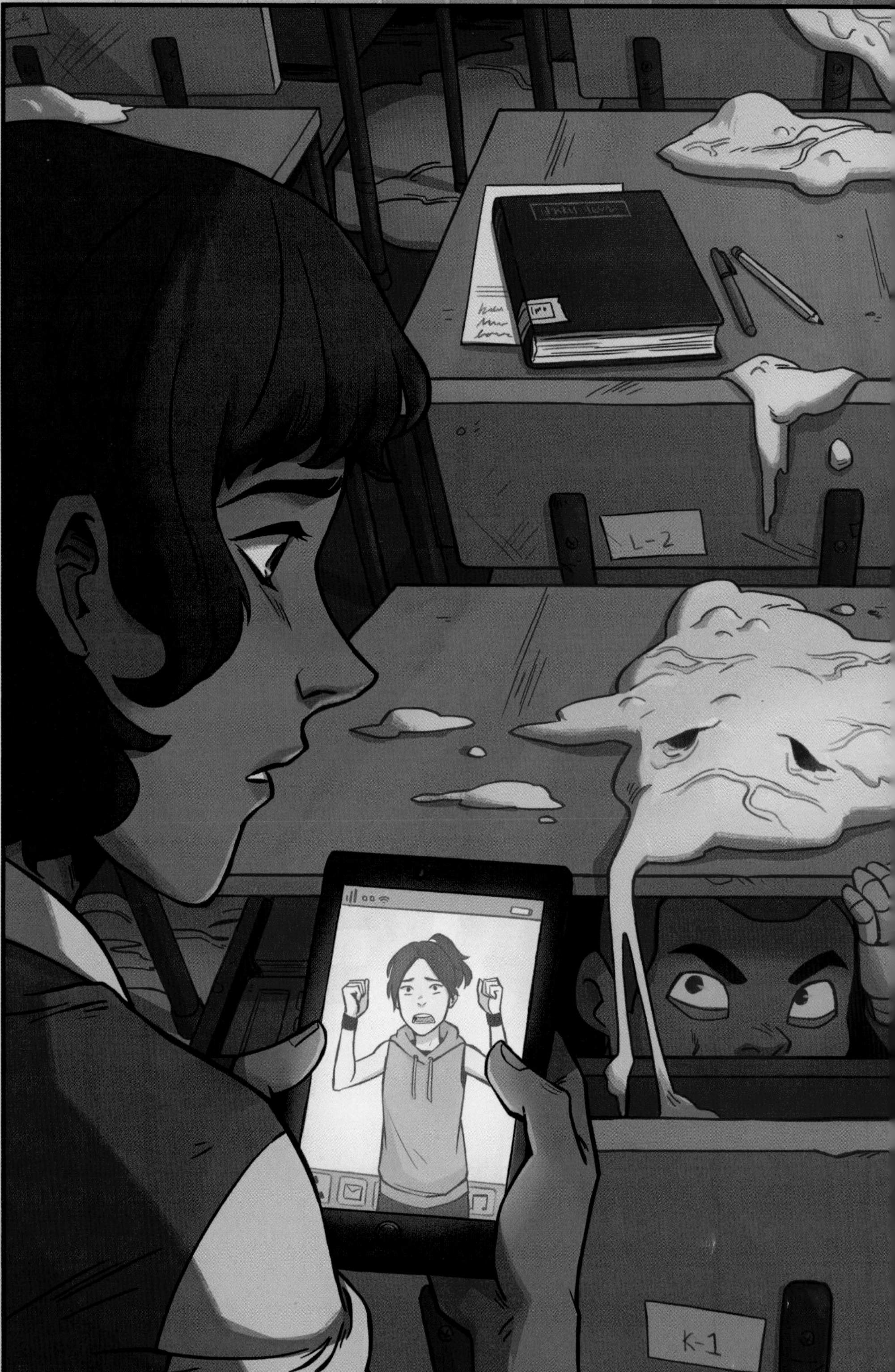
L-2
K-1

ART BY
MICHELLE WONG

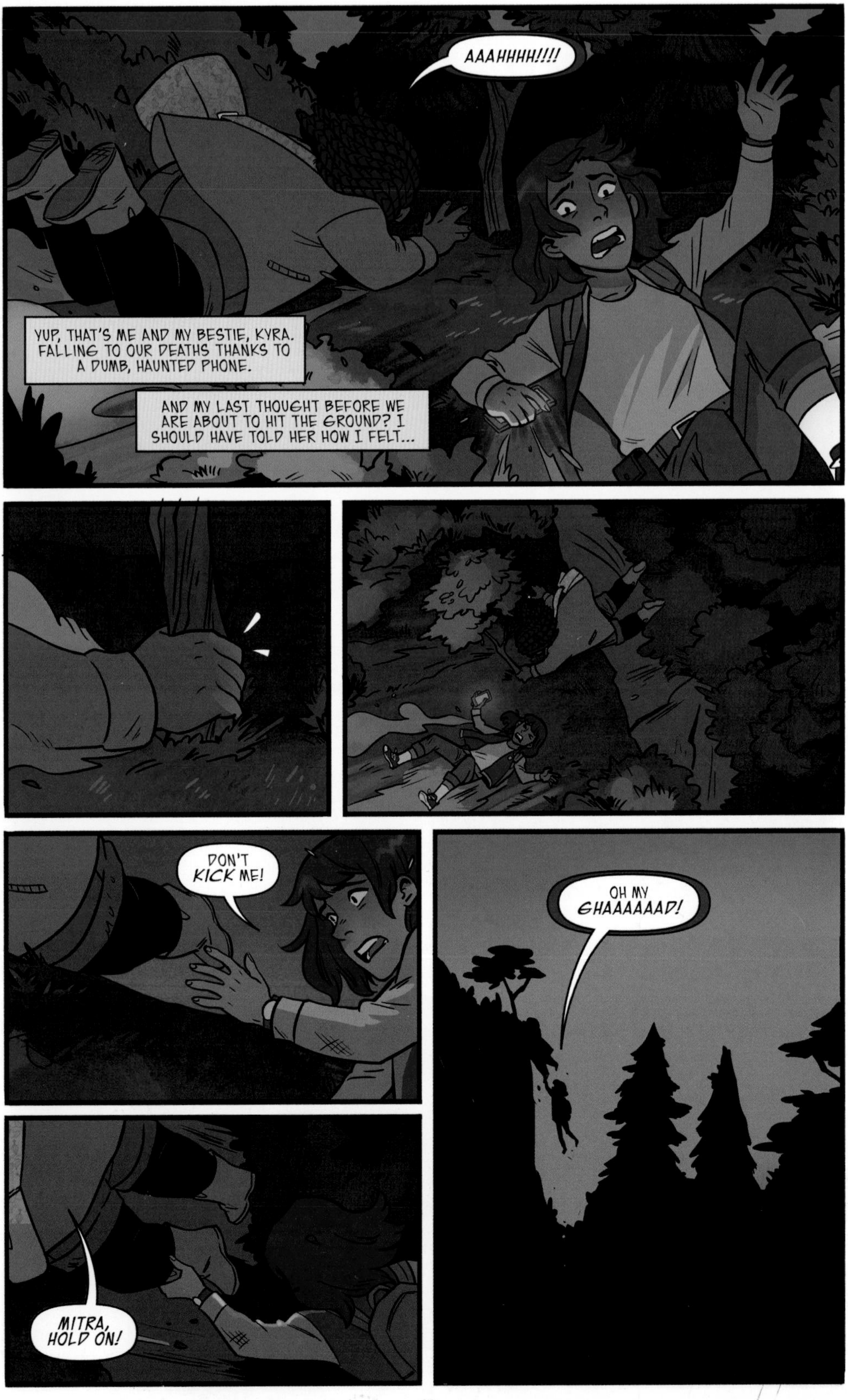
AAAHHHH!!!!
YUP, THAT'S ME AND MY BESTIE, KYRA. FALLING TO OUR DEATHS THANKS TO A DUMB, HAUNTED PHONE.
AND MY LAST THOUGHT BEFORE WE ARE ABOUT TO HIT THE GROUND? I SHOULD HAVE TOLD HER HOW I FELT...
DON'T KICK ME!
MITRA, HOLD ON!
OH MY GHAAAAAAD!

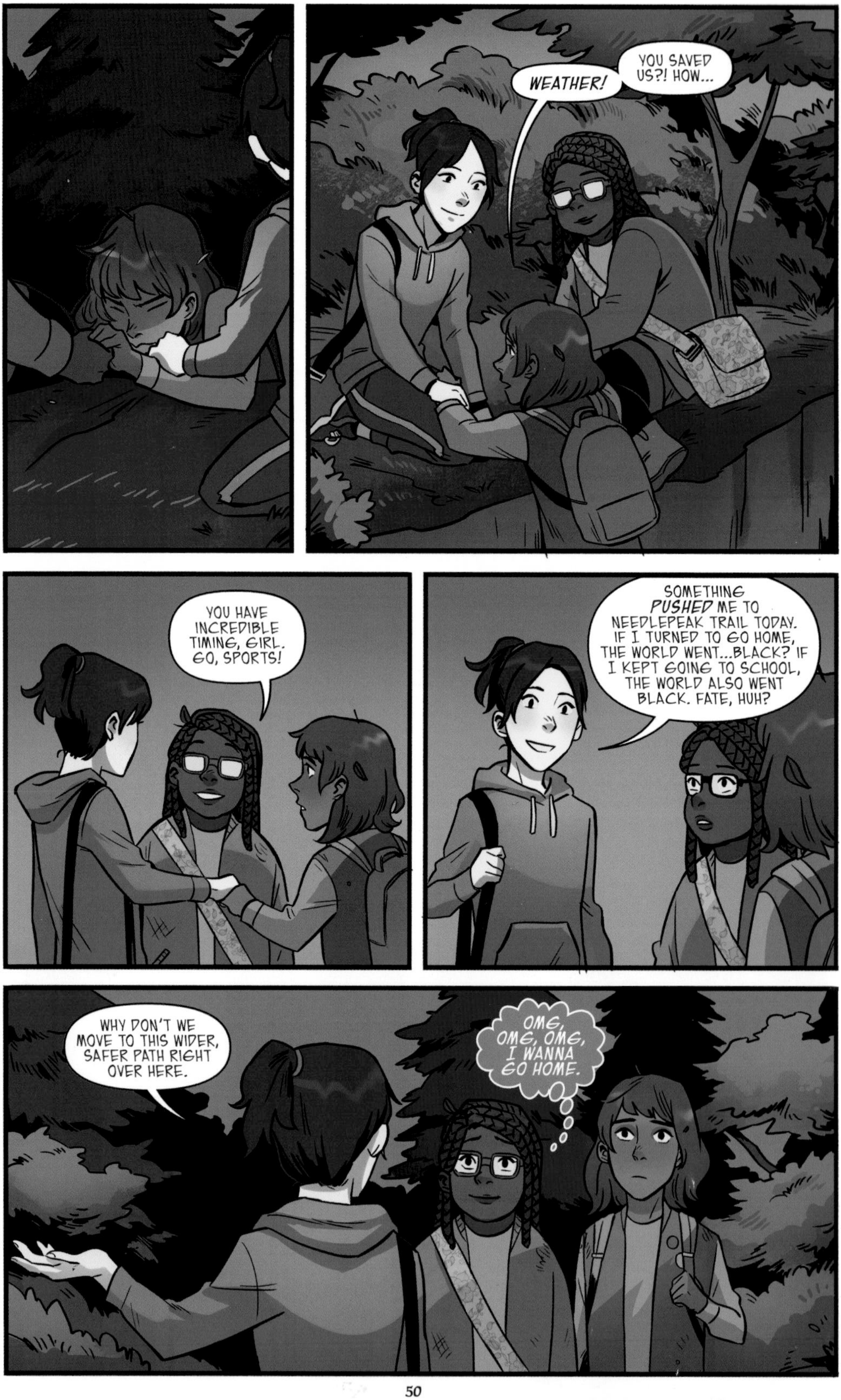

WEATHER!
YOU SAVED US?! HOW...
YOU HAVE INCREDIBLE TIMING, GIRL. GO, SPORTS!
SOMETHING *PUSHED* ME TO NEEDLEPEAK TRAIL TODAY. IF I TURNED TO GO HOME, THE WORLD WENT...BLACK? IF I KEPT GOING TO SCHOOL, THE WORLD ALSO WENT BLACK. FATE, HUH?
WHY DON'T WE MOVE TO THIS WIDER, SAFER PATH RIGHT OVER HERE.
OMG, OMG, OMG, I WANNA GO HOME.

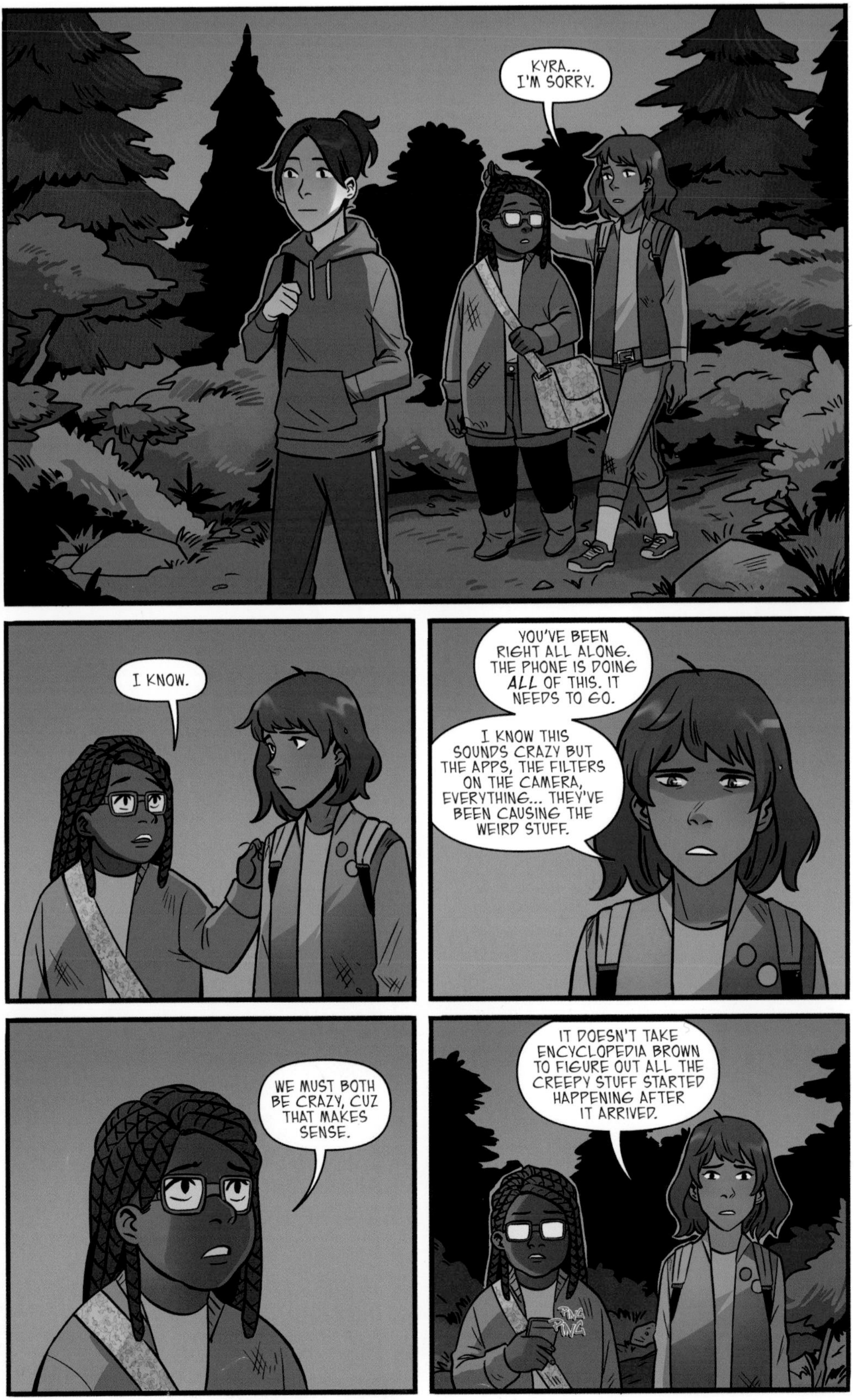
KYRA... I'M SORRY.
I KNOW.
YOU'VE BEEN RIGHT ALL ALONG. THE PHONE IS DOING *ALL* OF THIS. IT NEEDS TO GO.
I KNOW THIS SOUNDS CRAZY BUT THE APPS, THE FILTERS ON THE CAMERA, EVERYTHING... THEY'VE BEEN CAUSING THE WEIRD STUFF.
WE MUST BOTH BE CRAZY, CUZ THAT MAKES SENSE.
IT DOESN'T TAKE ENCYCLOPEDIA BROWN TO FIGURE OUT ALL THE CREEPY STUFF STARTED HAPPENING AFTER IT ARRIVED.
PING PING

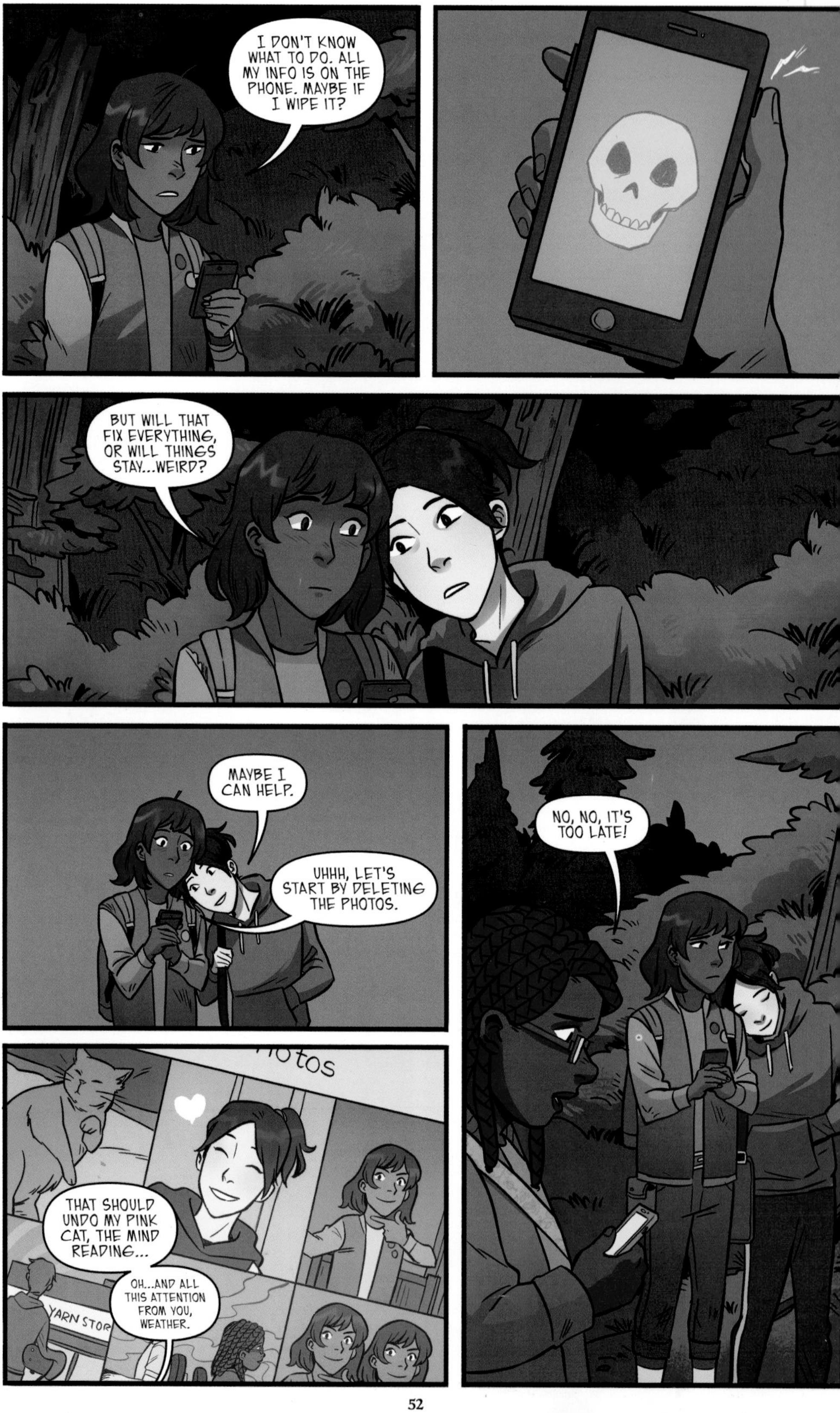
I DON'T KNOW WHAT TO DO. ALL MY INFO IS ON THE PHONE. MAYBE IF I WIPE IT?
BUT WILL THAT FIX EVERYTHING, OR WILL THINGS STAY...WEIRD?
MAYBE I CAN HELP.
UHHH, LET'S START BY DELETING THE PHOTOS.
otos
THAT SHOULD UNDO MY PINK CAT, THE MIND READING...
OH...AND ALL THIS ATTENTION FROM YOU, WEATHER.
YARN STOR
NO, NO, IT'S TOO LATE!

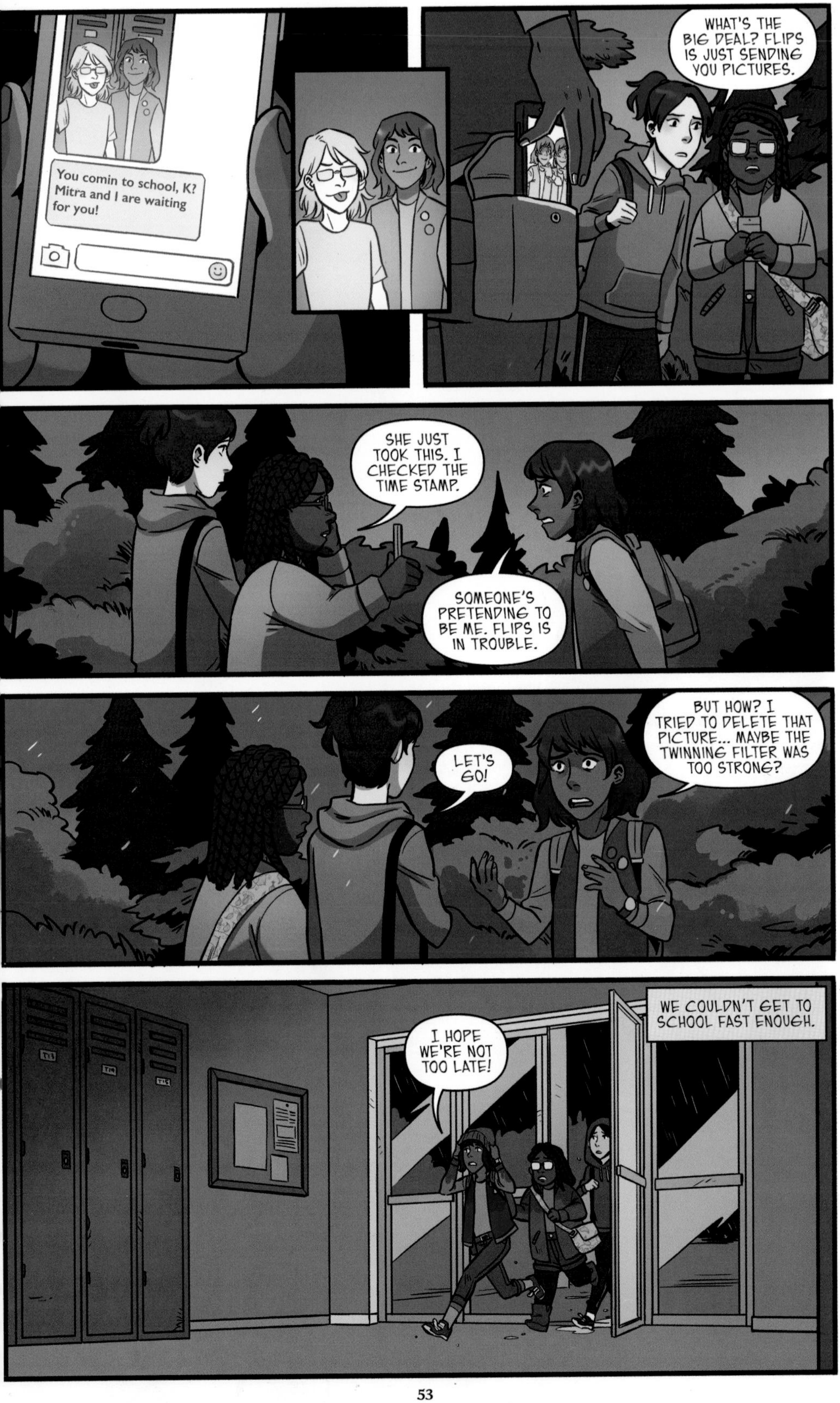
You comin to school, K? Mitra and I are waiting for you!
WHAT'S THE BIG DEAL? FLIPS IS JUST SENDING YOU PICTURES.
SHE JUST TOOK THIS. I CHECKED THE TIME STAMP.
SOMEONE'S PRETENDING TO BE ME. FLIPS IS IN TROUBLE.
LET'S GO!
BUT HOW? I TRIED TO DELETE THAT PICTURE... MAYBE THE TWINNING FILTER WAS TOO STRONG?
WE COULDN'T GET TO SCHOOL FAST ENOUGH.
I HOPE WE'RE NOT TOO LATE!

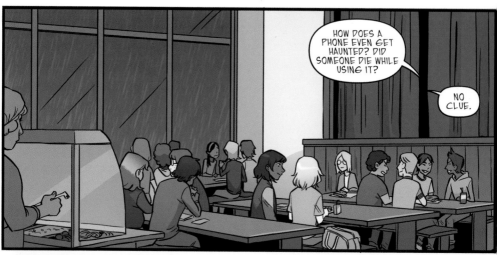

HOW DOES A PHONE EVEN GET HAUNTED? DID SOMEONE DIE WHILE USING IT?

NO CLUE.

DO I REALLY USE MY HANDS LIKE THAT?

MITRA!

OH, RIGHT. LET'S TRY TEXTING HER.

WHY DIDN'T I THINK OF THAT!

READ THE PHONE!

OOPSIE DAISY...

DEAR ME, LADIES, WHAT'S THE DRAMA? ANY HOT GOSS?

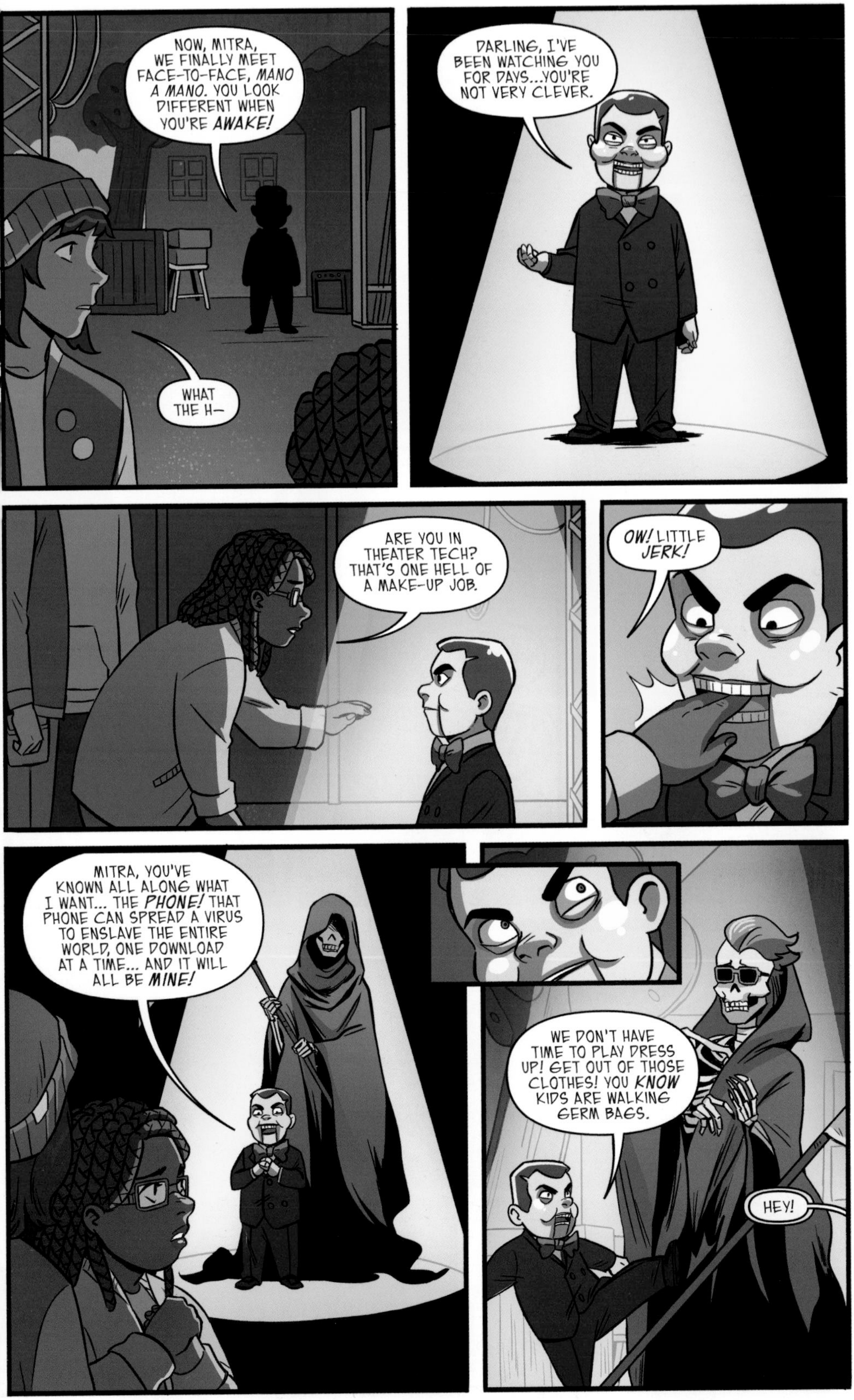
NOW, MITRA, WE FINALLY MEET FACE-TO-FACE, MANO A MANO. YOU LOOK DIFFERENT WHEN YOU'RE AWAKE!
WHAT THE H—
DARLING, I'VE BEEN WATCHING YOU FOR DAYS...YOU'RE NOT VERY CLEVER.
ARE YOU IN THEATER TECH? THAT'S ONE HELL OF A MAKE-UP JOB.
OW! LITTLE JERK!
MITRA, YOU'VE KNOWN ALL ALONG WHAT I WANT... THE PHONE! THAT PHONE CAN SPREAD A VIRUS TO ENSLAVE THE ENTIRE WORLD, ONE DOWNLOAD AT A TIME... AND IT WILL ALL BE MINE!
WE DON'T HAVE TIME TO PLAY DRESS UP! GET OUT OF THOSE CLOTHES! YOU KNOW KIDS ARE WALKING GERM BAGS.
HEY!

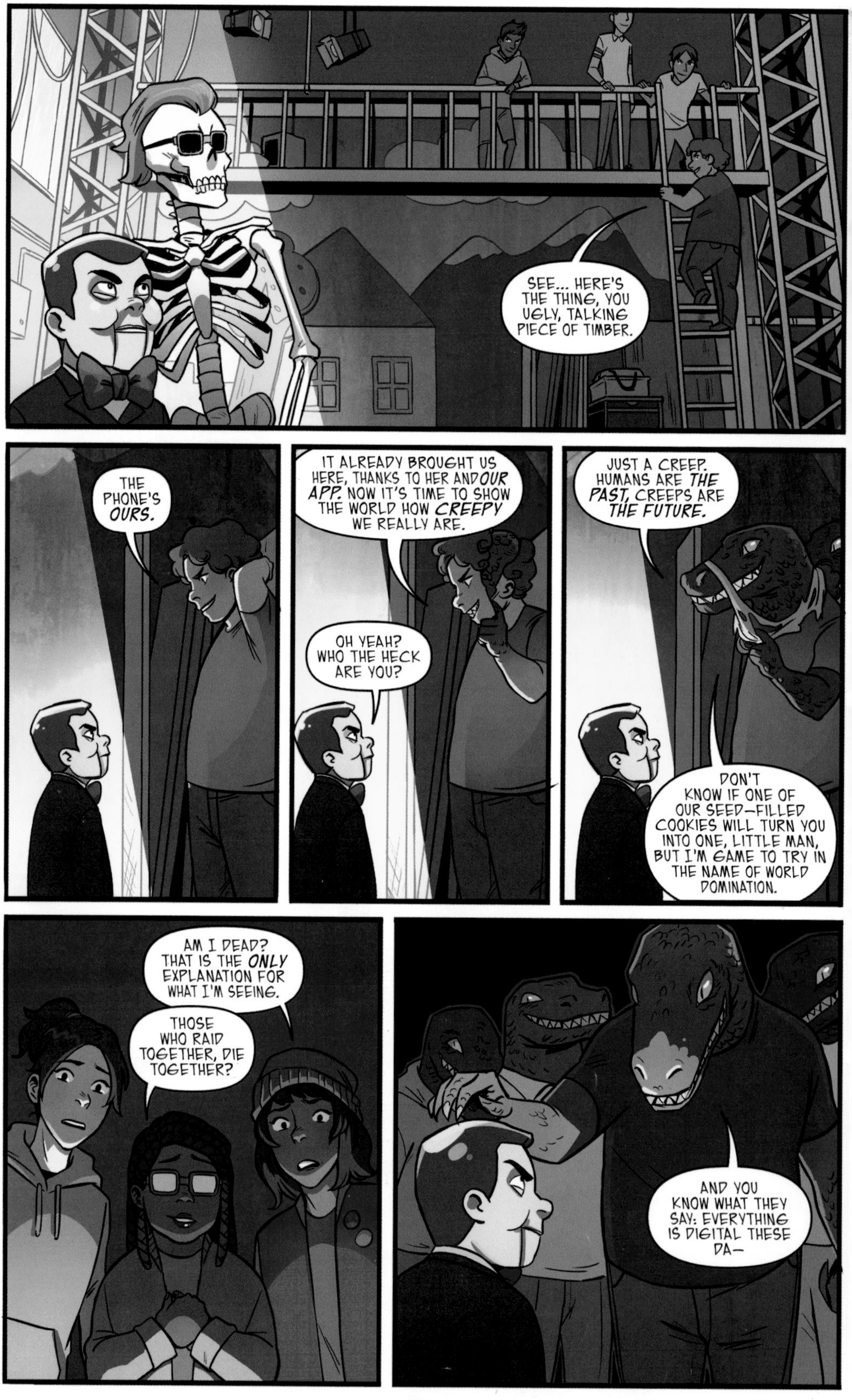

SEE... HERE'S THE THING, YOU UGLY, TALKING PIECE OF TIMBER.
THE PHONE'S *OURS.*
IT ALREADY BROUGHT US HERE, THANKS TO HER AND *OUR APP.* NOW IT'S TIME TO SHOW THE WORLD HOW *CREEPY* WE REALLY ARE.
OH YEAH? WHO THE HECK ARE YOU?
JUST A CREEP. HUMANS ARE *THE PAST,* CREEPS ARE *THE FUTURE.*
DON'T KNOW IF ONE OF OUR SEED-FILLED COOKIES WILL TURN YOU INTO ONE, LITTLE MAN, BUT I'M GAME TO TRY IN THE NAME OF WORLD DOMINATION.
AM I DEAD? THAT IS THE *ONLY* EXPLANATION FOR WHAT I'M SEEING.
THOSE WHO RAID TOGETHER, DIE TOGETHER?
AND YOU KNOW WHAT THEY SAY: EVERYTHING IS DIGITAL THESE DA—

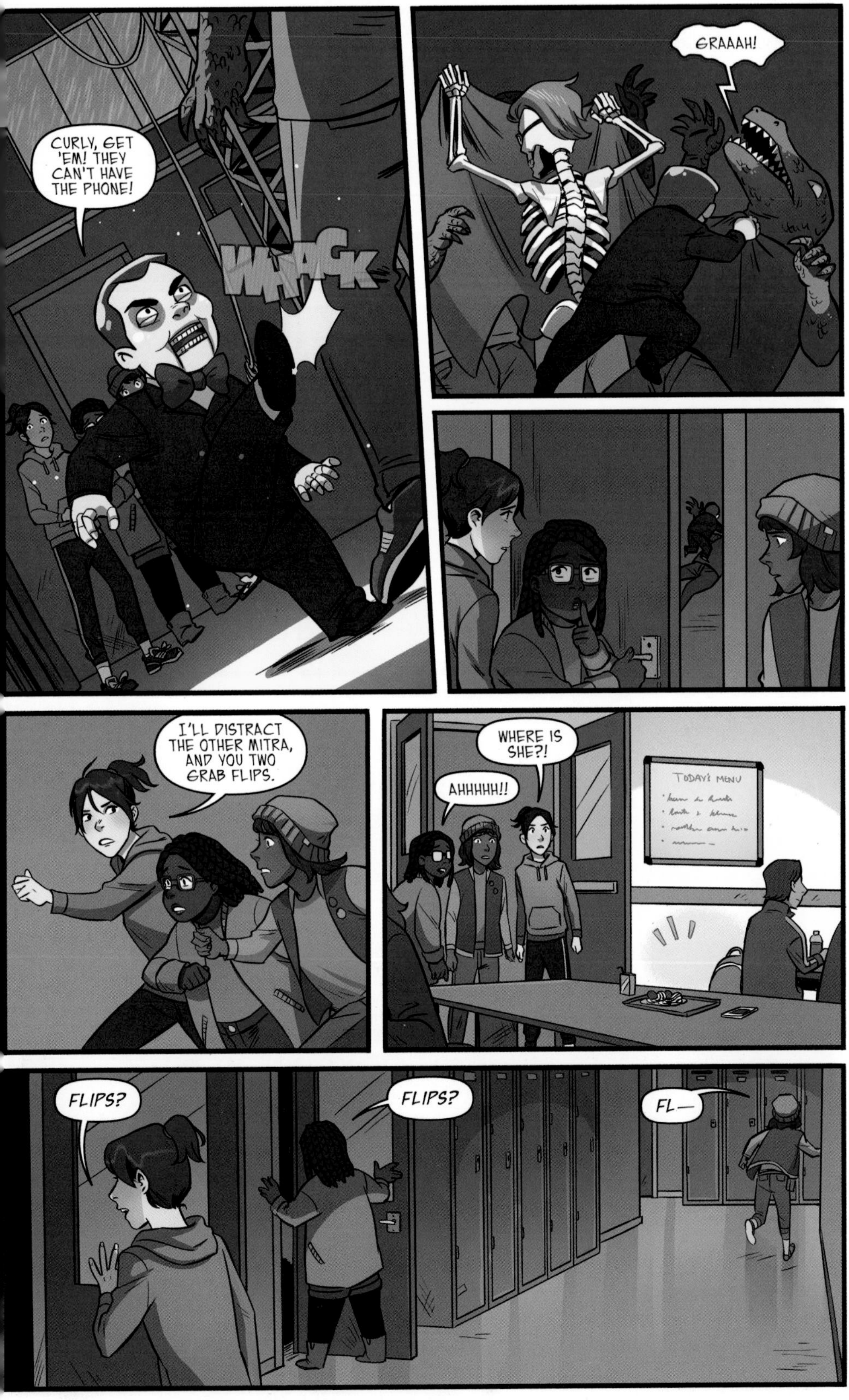
CURLY, GET 'EM! THEY CAN'T HAVE THE PHONE!
WHACK
GRAAAH!
I'LL DISTRACT THE OTHER MITRA, AND YOU TWO GRAB FLIPS.
WHERE IS SHE?!
AHHHHH!!
TODAY'S MENU
FLIPS?
FLIPS?
FL—

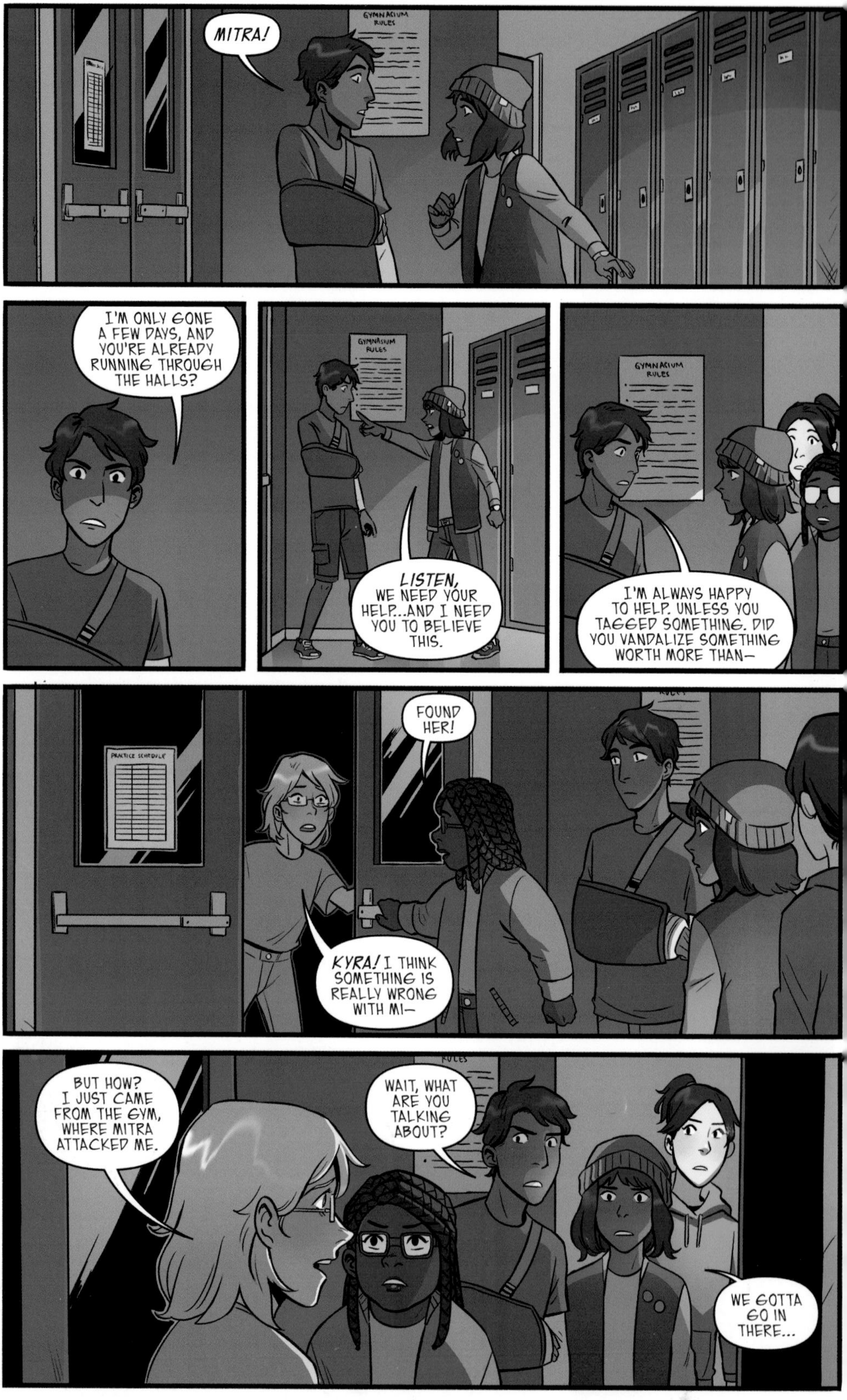
MITRA!
GYMNASIUM RULES
I'M ONLY GONE A FEW DAYS, AND YOU'RE ALREADY RUNNING THROUGH THE HALLS?
GYMNASIUM RULES
LISTEN, WE NEED YOUR HELP...AND I NEED YOU TO BELIEVE THIS.
GYMNASIUM RULES
I'M ALWAYS HAPPY TO HELP. UNLESS YOU TAGGED SOMETHING. DID YOU VANDALIZE SOMETHING WORTH MORE THAN—
PRACTICE SCHEDULE
FOUND HER!
KYRA! I THINK SOMETHING IS REALLY WRONG WITH MI—
BUT HOW? I JUST CAME FROM THE GYM, WHERE MITRA ATTACKED ME.
WAIT, WHAT ARE YOU TALKING ABOUT?
WE GOTTA GO IN THERE...

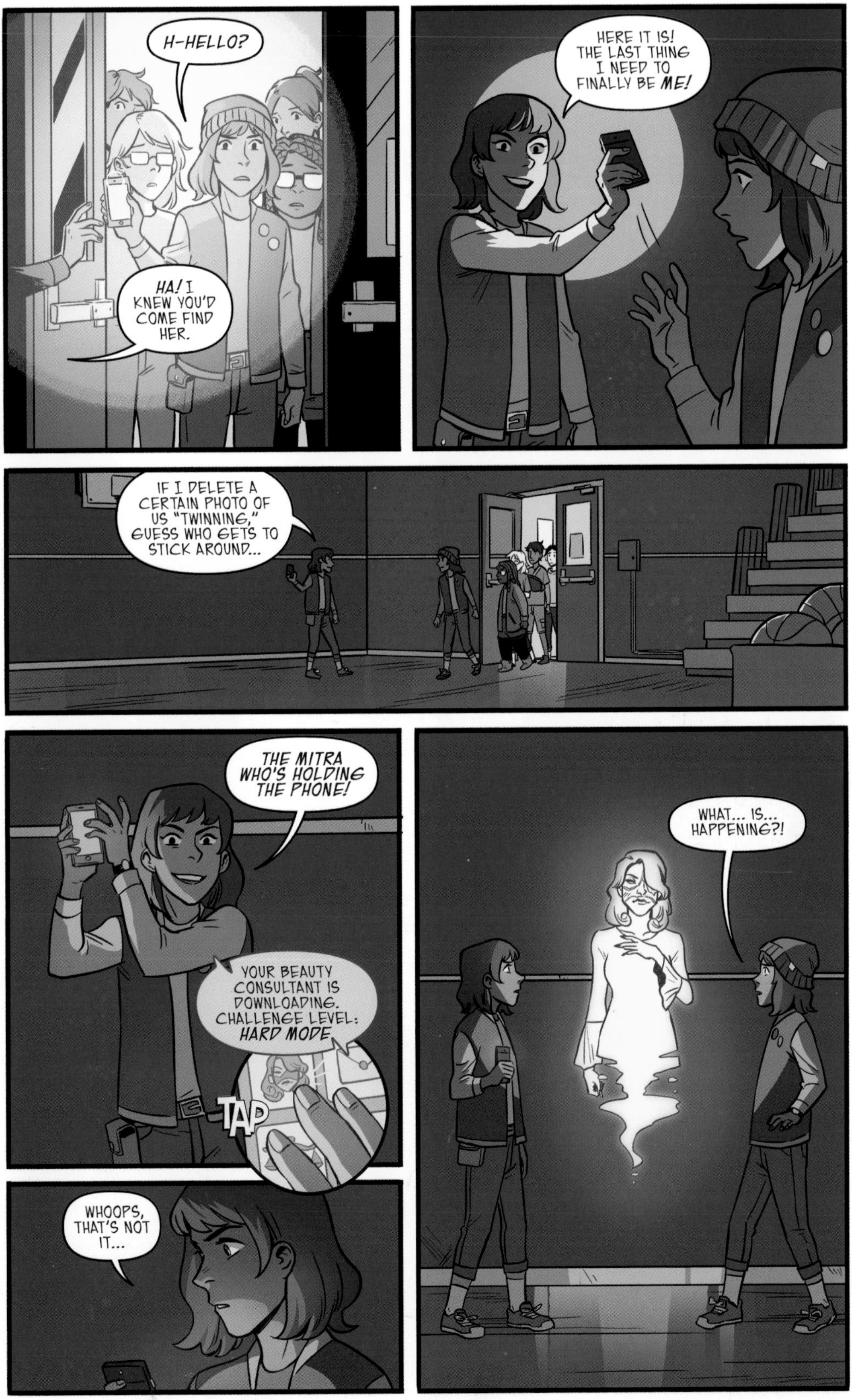
H-HELLO?
HA! I KNEW YOU'D COME FIND HER.
HERE IT IS! THE LAST THING I NEED TO FINALLY BE ME!
IF I DELETE A CERTAIN PHOTO OF US "TWINNING," GUESS WHO GETS TO STICK AROUND...
THE MITRA WHO'S HOLDING THE PHONE!
YOUR BEAUTY CONSULTANT IS DOWNLOADING. CHALLENGE LEVEL: HARD MODE
TAP
WHOOPS, THAT'S NOT IT...
WHAT... IS... HAPPENING?!

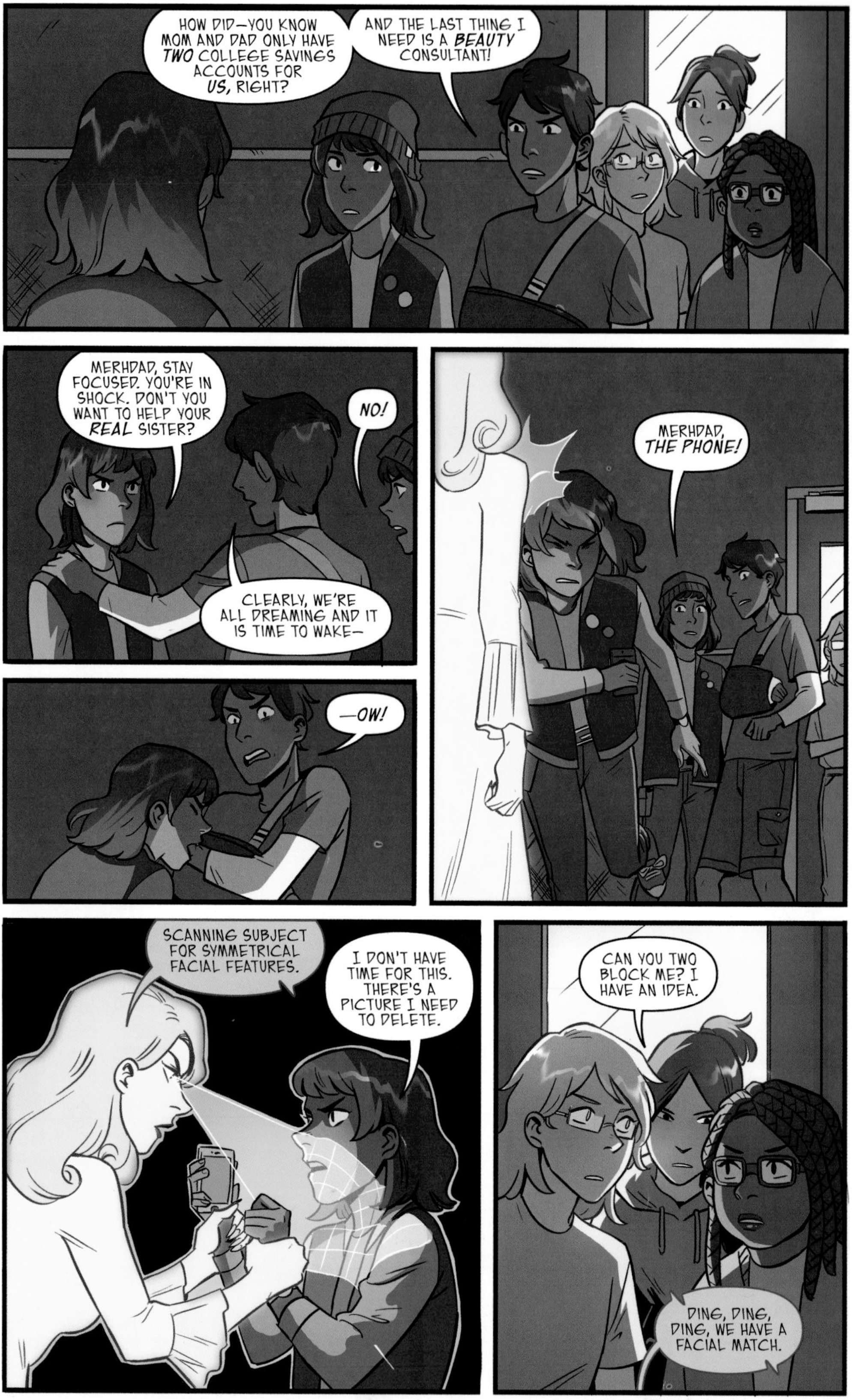

HOW DID—YOU KNOW MOM AND DAD ONLY HAVE TWO COLLEGE SAVINGS ACCOUNTS FOR US, RIGHT?
AND THE LAST THING I NEED IS A BEAUTY CONSULTANT!
MERHDAD, STAY FOCUSED. YOU'RE IN SHOCK. DON'T YOU WANT TO HELP YOUR REAL SISTER?
NO!
CLEARLY, WE'RE ALL DREAMING AND IT IS TIME TO WAKE—
—OW!
MERHDAD, THE PHONE!
SCANNING SUBJECT FOR SYMMETRICAL FACIAL FEATURES.
I DON'T HAVE TIME FOR THIS. THERE'S A PICTURE I NEED TO DELETE.
CAN YOU TWO BLOCK ME? I HAVE AN IDEA.
DING, DING, DING, WE HAVE A FACIAL MATCH.

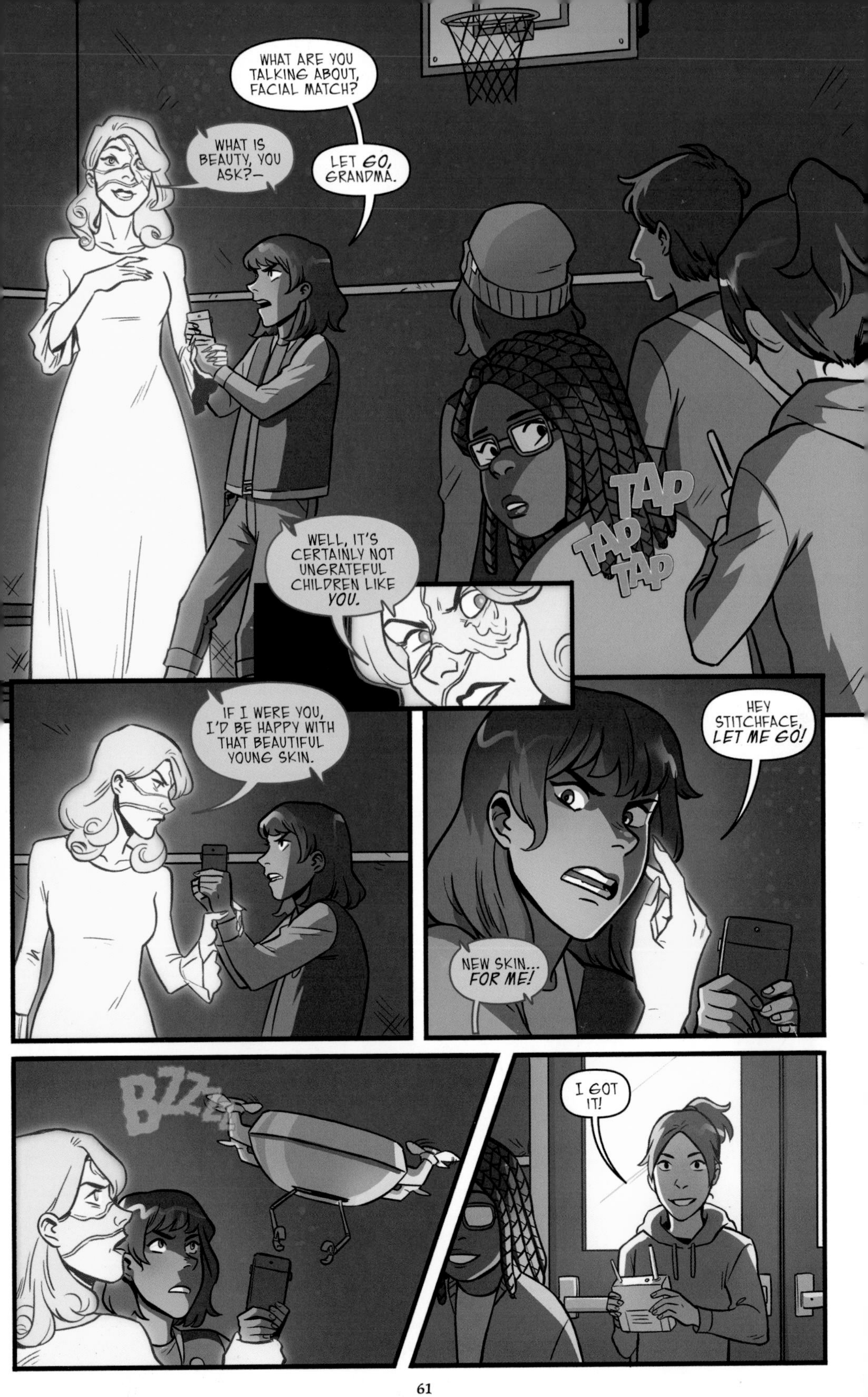
WHAT ARE YOU TALKING ABOUT, FACIAL MATCH?
WHAT IS BEAUTY, YOU ASK?—
LET GO, GRANDMA.
TAP
TAP
TAP
WELL, IT'S CERTAINLY NOT UNGRATEFUL CHILDREN LIKE YOU.
IF I WERE YOU, I'D BE HAPPY WITH THAT BEAUTIFUL YOUNG SKIN.
HEY STITCHFACE, LET ME GO!
NEW SKIN... FOR ME!
BZZZ
I GOT IT!

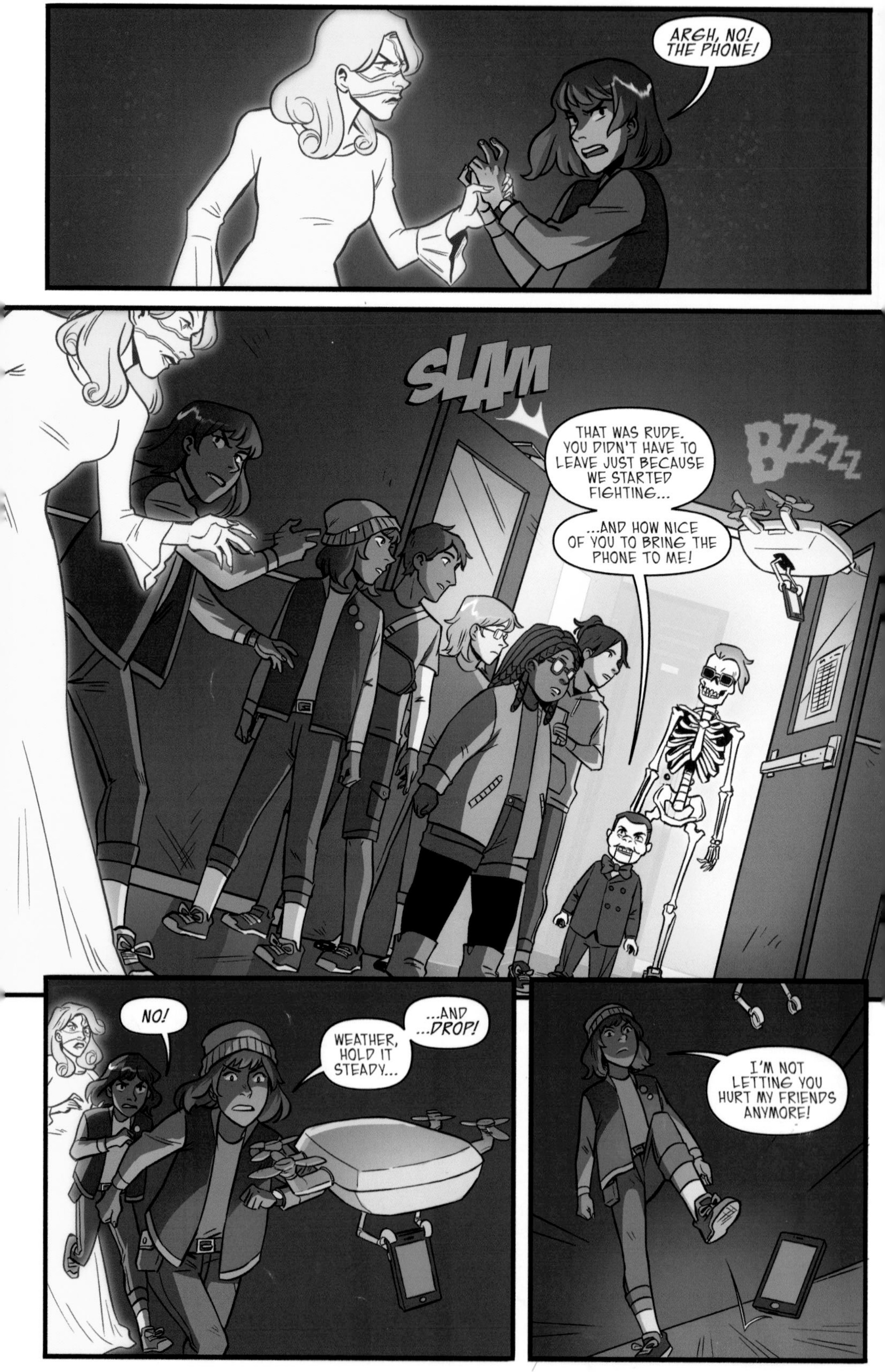
ARGH, NO! THE PHONE!
SLAM
BZZZZZ
THAT WAS RUDE. YOU DIDN'T HAVE TO LEAVE JUST BECAUSE WE STARTED FIGHTING...
...AND HOW NICE OF YOU TO BRING THE PHONE TO ME!
NO!
WEATHER, HOLD IT STEADY...
...AND ...DROP!
I'M NOT LETTING YOU HURT MY FRIENDS ANYMORE!

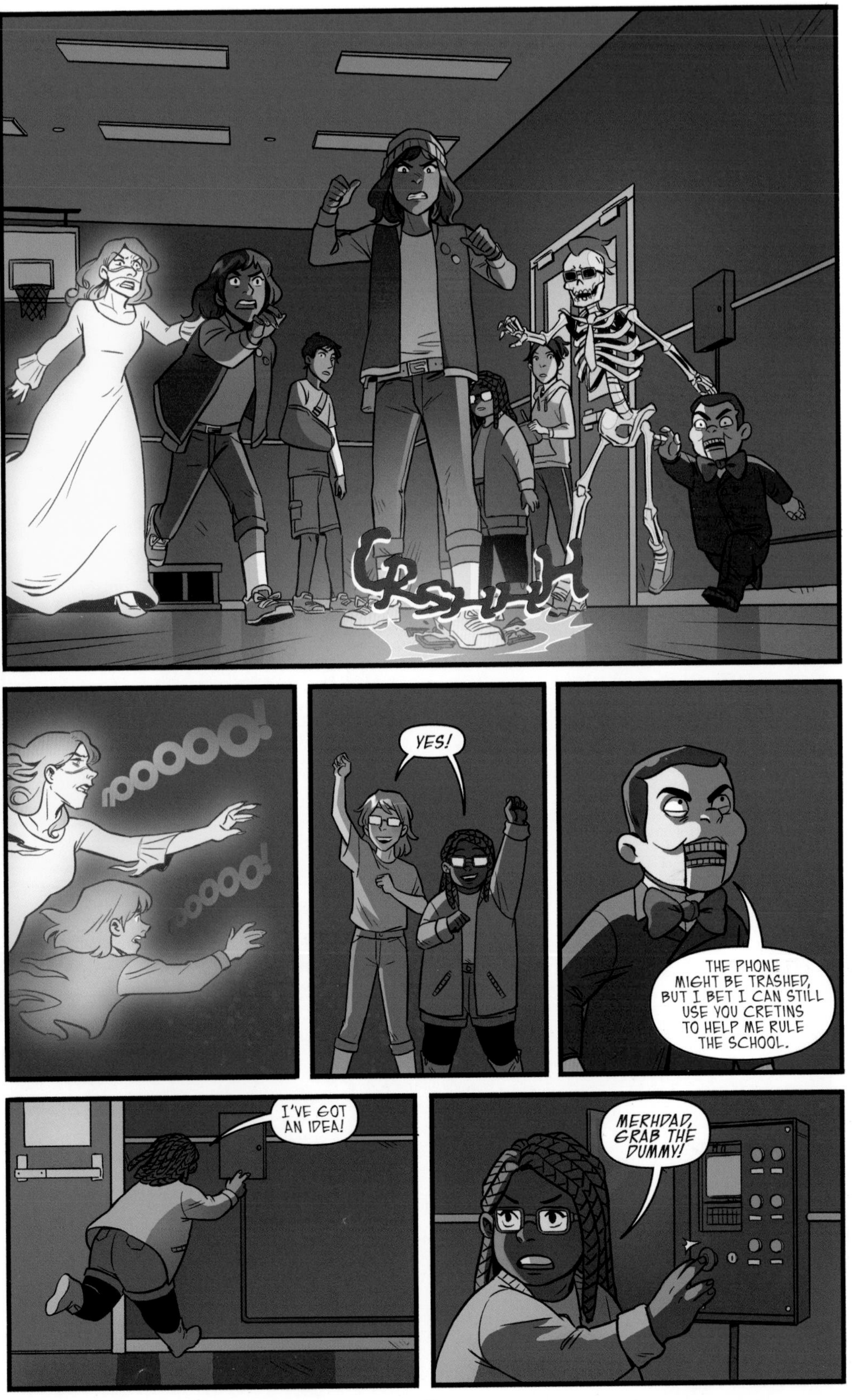
CRSHHH
NOOOOO!
NOOOOO!
YES!
THE PHONE MIGHT BE TRASHED, BUT I BET I CAN STILL USE YOU CRETINS TO HELP ME RULE THE SCHOOL.
I'VE GOT AN IDEA!
MERHDAD, GRAB THE DUMMY!

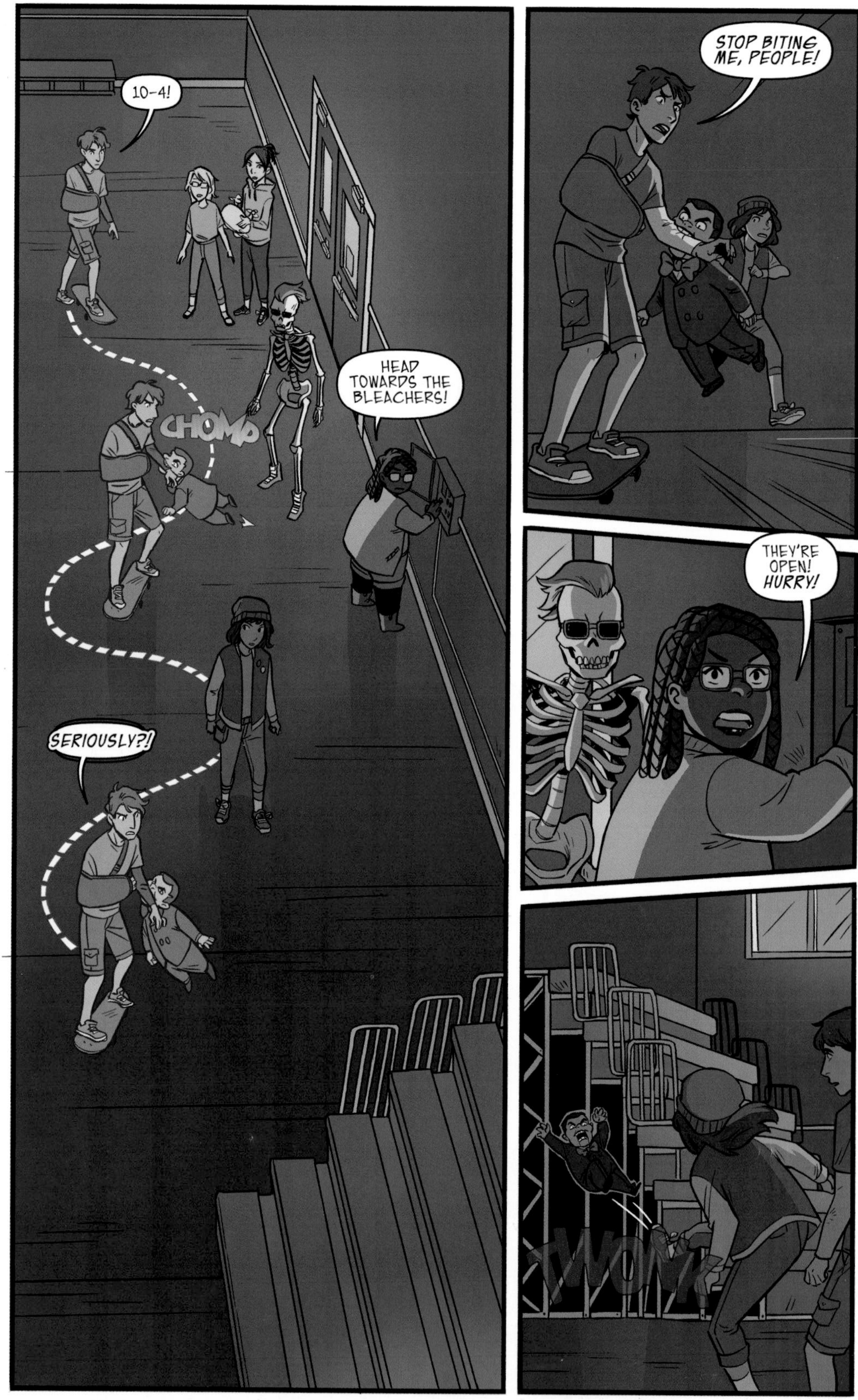
10-4!
HEAD TOWARDS THE BLEACHERS!
CHOMP
SERIOUSLY?!
STOP BITING ME, PEOPLE!
THEY'RE OPEN! HURRY!
TWOMP

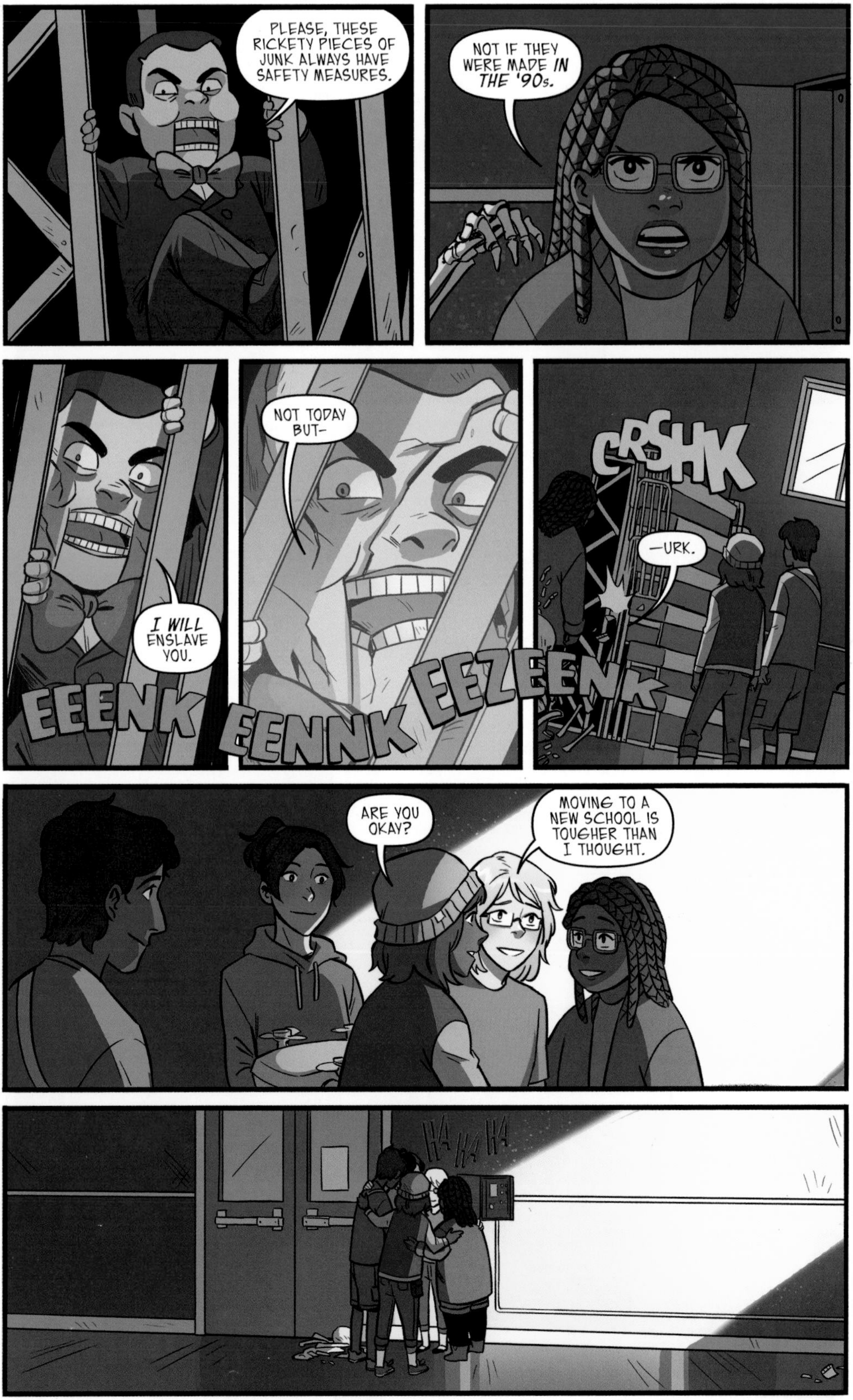
PLEASE, THESE RICKETY PIECES OF JUNK ALWAYS HAVE SAFETY MEASURES.
NOT IF THEY WERE MADE *IN THE '90s.*
I WILL ENSLAVE YOU.
NOT TODAY BUT–
EEEENK
EENNK
EEZEENK
CRSHK
—URK.
ARE YOU OKAY?
MOVING TO A NEW SCHOOL IS TOUGHER THAN I THOUGHT.
HA HA HA!

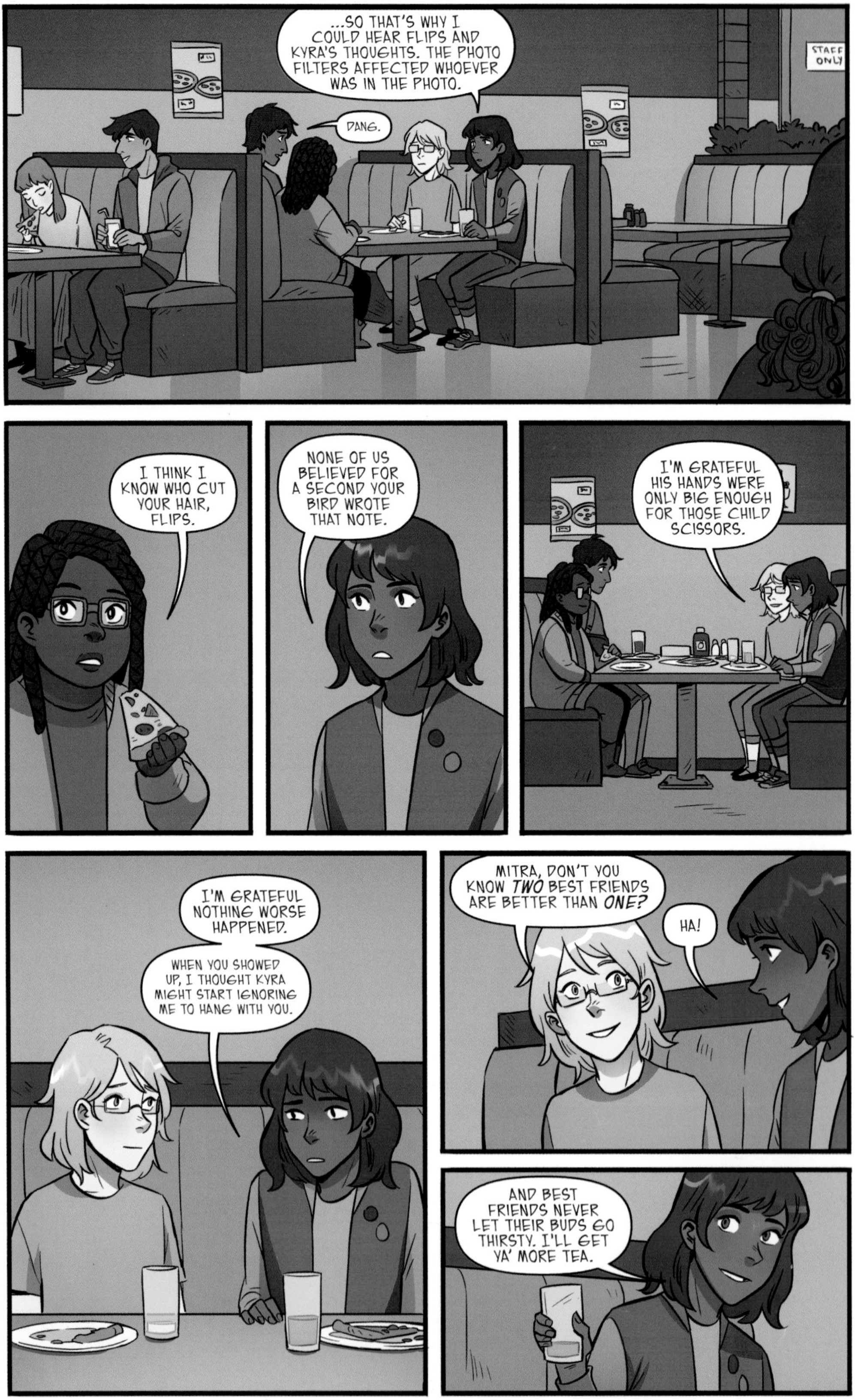

...SO THAT'S WHY I COULD HEAR FLIPS AND KYRA'S THOUGHTS. THE PHOTO FILTERS AFFECTED WHOEVER WAS IN THE PHOTO.
DANG.
STAFF ONLY
I THINK I KNOW WHO CUT YOUR HAIR, FLIPS.
NONE OF US BELIEVED FOR A SECOND YOUR BIRD WROTE THAT NOTE.
I'M GRATEFUL HIS HANDS WERE ONLY BIG ENOUGH FOR THOSE CHILD SCISSORS.
I'M GRATEFUL NOTHING WORSE HAPPENED.
WHEN YOU SHOWED UP, I THOUGHT KYRA MIGHT START IGNORING ME TO HANG WITH YOU.
MITRA, DON'T YOU KNOW *TWO* BEST FRIENDS ARE BETTER THAN *ONE?*
HA!
AND BEST FRIENDS NEVER LET THEIR BUDS GO THIRSTY. I'LL GET YA' MORE TEA.

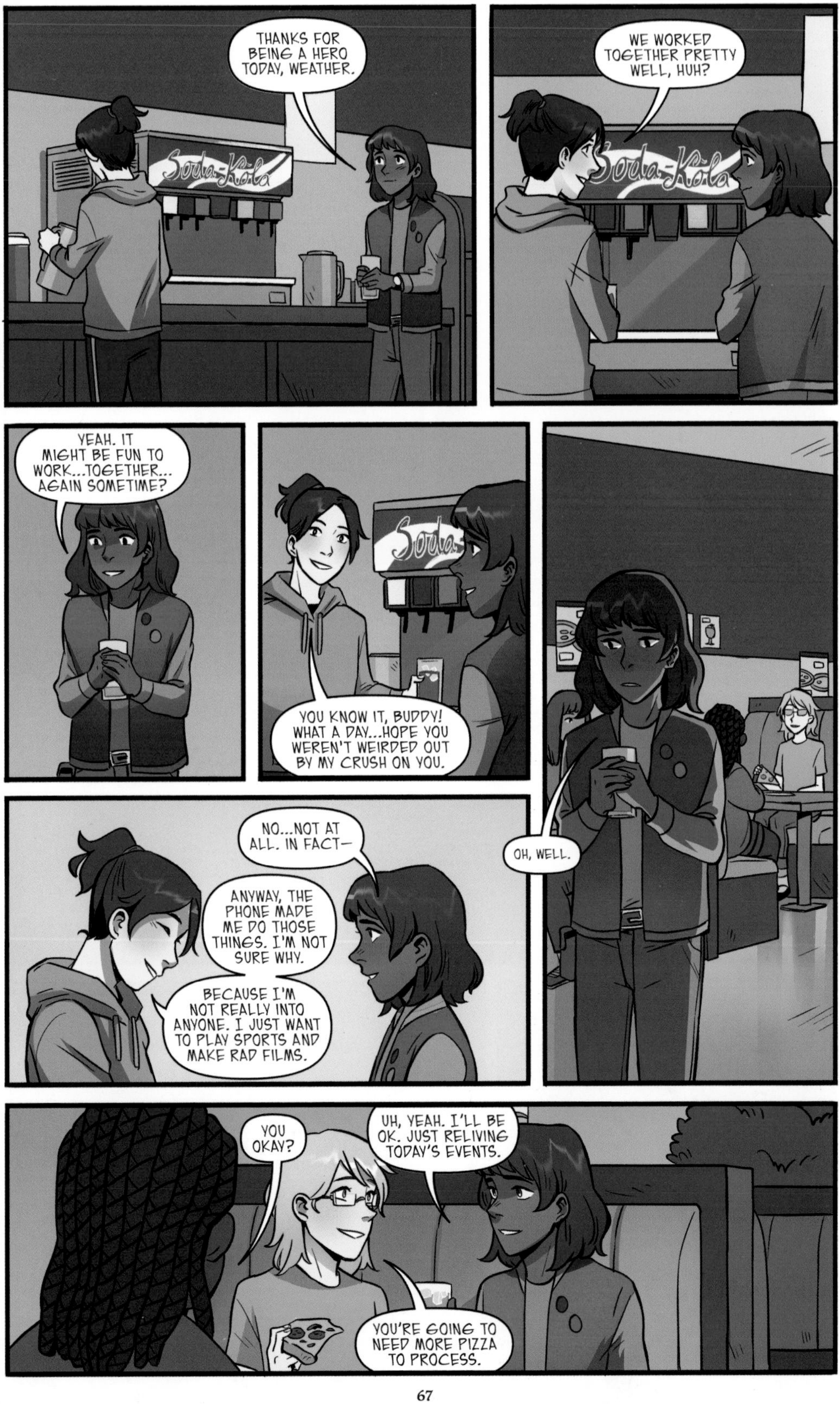
THANKS FOR BEING A HERO TODAY, WEATHER.
Soda-Kola
WE WORKED TOGETHER PRETTY WELL, HUH?
Soda-Kola
YEAH. IT MIGHT BE FUN TO WORK...TOGETHER... AGAIN SOMETIME?
Soda-
YOU KNOW IT, BUDDY! WHAT A DAY...HOPE YOU WEREN'T WEIRDED OUT BY MY CRUSH ON YOU.
NO...NOT AT ALL. IN FACT—
ANYWAY, THE PHONE MADE ME DO THOSE THINGS. I'M NOT SURE WHY.
BECAUSE I'M NOT REALLY INTO ANYONE. I JUST WANT TO PLAY SPORTS AND MAKE RAD FILMS.
OH, WELL.
YOU OKAY?
UH, YEAH. I'LL BE OK. JUST RELIVING TODAY'S EVENTS.
YOU'RE GOING TO NEED MORE PIZZA TO PROCESS.

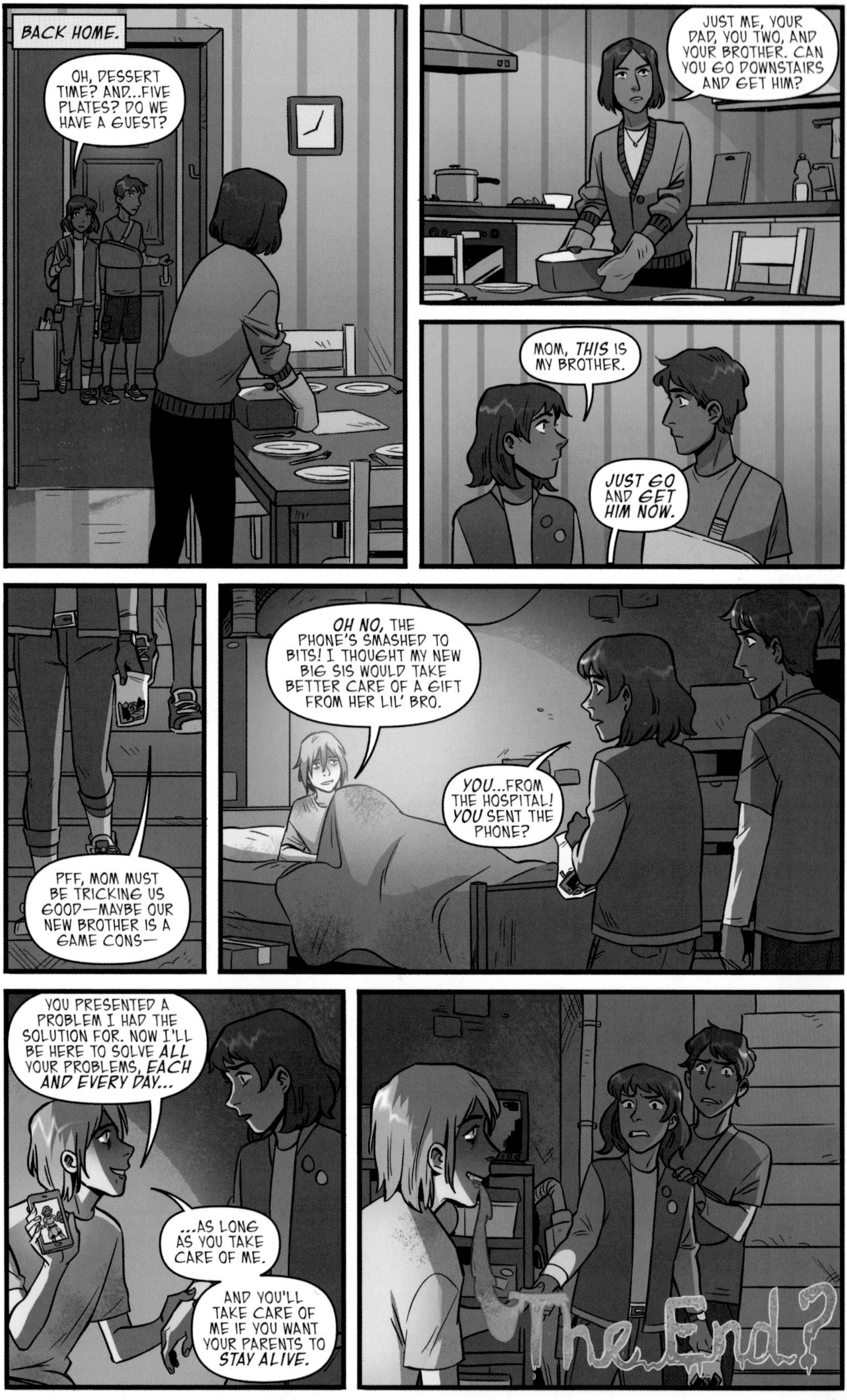
BACK HOME.
OH, DESSERT TIME? AND...FIVE PLATES? DO WE HAVE A GUEST?
JUST ME, YOUR DAD, YOU TWO, AND YOUR BROTHER. CAN YOU GO DOWNSTAIRS AND GET HIM?
MOM, THIS IS MY BROTHER.
JUST GO AND GET HIM NOW.
PFF, MOM MUST BE TRICKING US GOOD—MAYBE OUR NEW BROTHER IS A GAME CONS—
OH NO, THE PHONE'S SMASHED TO BITS! I THOUGHT MY NEW BIG SIS WOULD TAKE BETTER CARE OF A GIFT FROM HER LIL' BRO.
YOU...FROM THE HOSPITAL! YOU SENT THE PHONE?
YOU PRESENTED A PROBLEM I HAD THE SOLUTION FOR. NOW I'LL BE HERE TO SOLVE ALL YOUR PROBLEMS, EACH AND EVERY DAY...
...AS LONG AS YOU TAKE CARE OF ME.
AND YOU'LL TAKE CARE OF ME IF YOU WANT YOUR PARENTS TO STAY ALIVE.
The End?

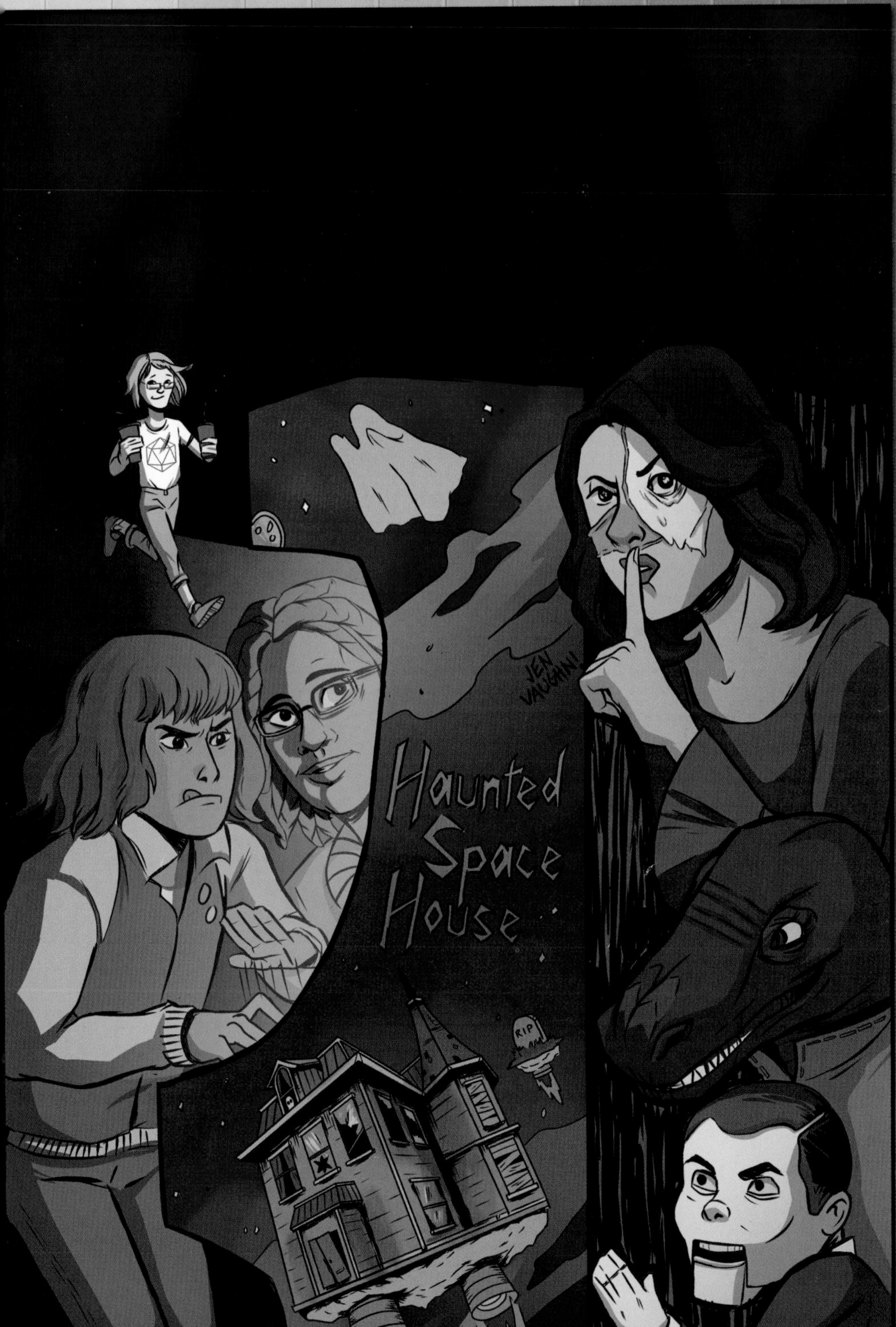
JEN VAUGHN!
Haunted Space House
RIP

ART BY
JEN VAUGHN

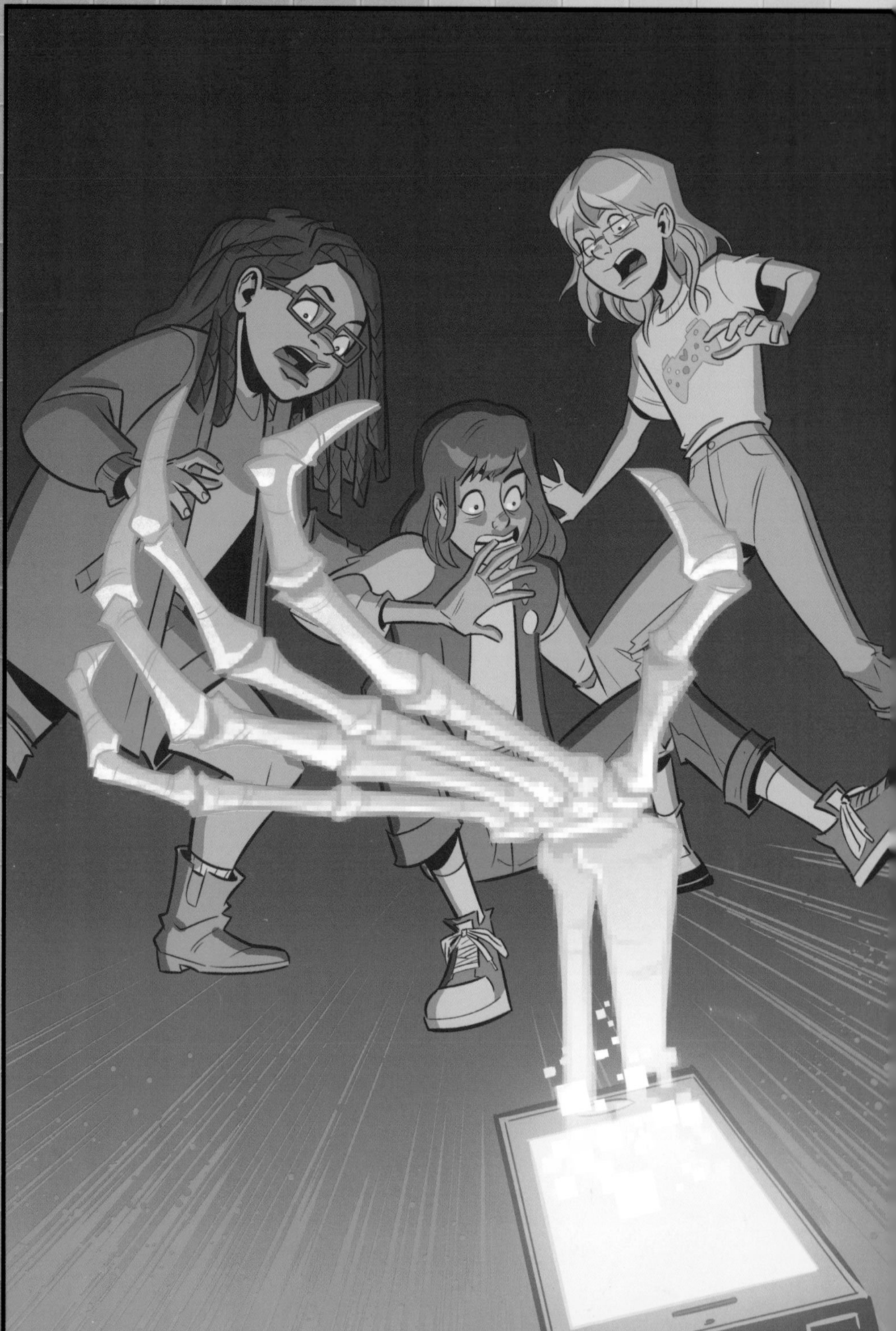
FENOGLIO

ART BY
CHRIS FENOGLIO

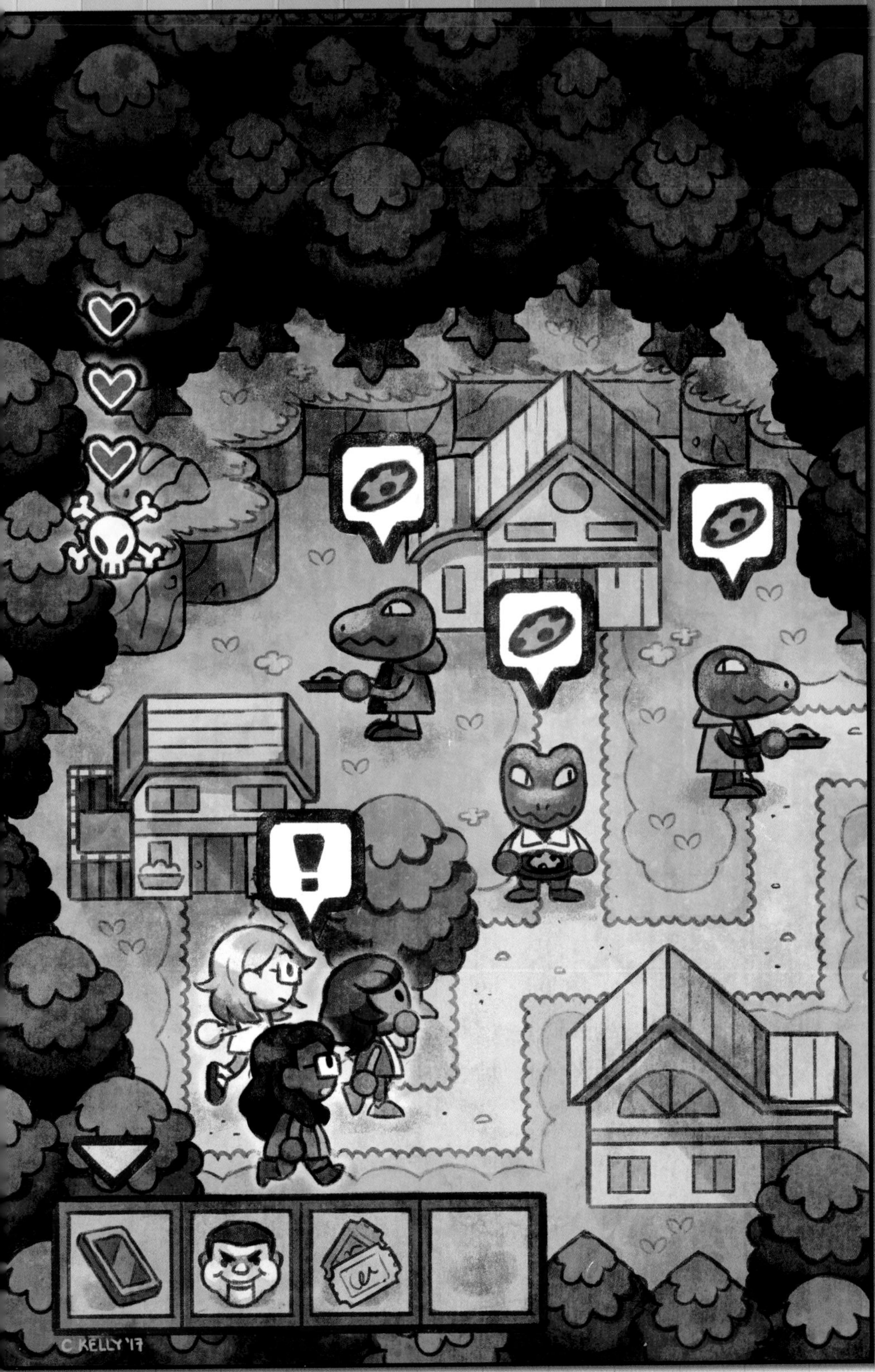

!
C KELLY '17

ART BY
CHRISTINA KELLY

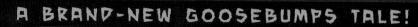

A BRAND-NEW GOOSEBUMPS TALE!

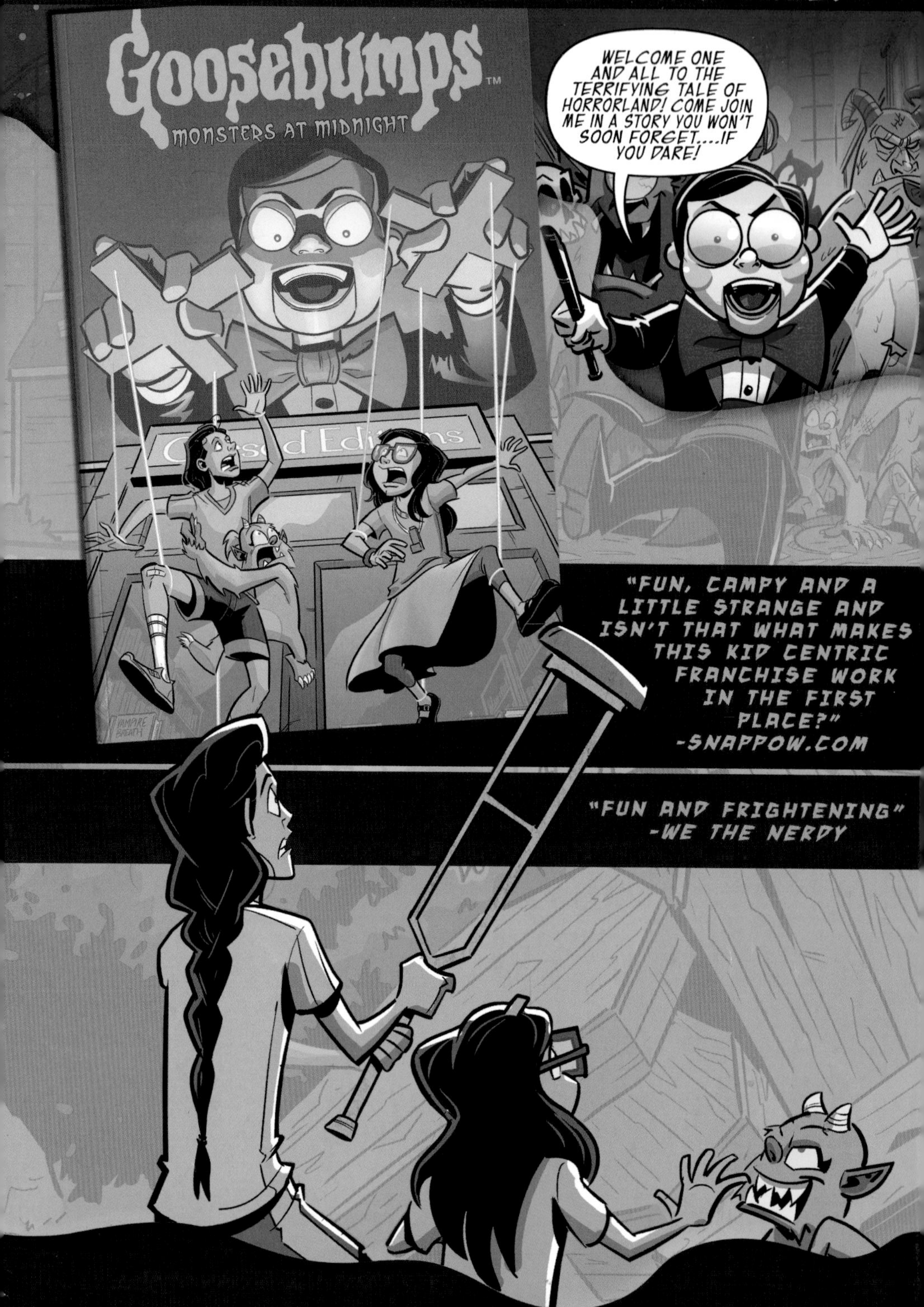

MONSTERS AT MIDNIGHT

Cursed Editions

WELCOME ONE AND ALL TO THE TERRIFYING TALE OF HORRORLAND! COME JOIN ME IN A STORY YOU WON'T SOON FORGET.....IF YOU DARE!

"FUN, CAMPY AND A LITTLE STRANGE AND ISN'T THAT WHAT MAKES THIS KID CENTRIC FRANCHISE WORK IN THE FIRST PLACE?"
-SNAPPOW.COM

"FUN AND FRIGHTENING"
-WE THE NERDY

JEREMY LAMBERT (W) · **CHRIS FENOGLIO** (A)
FULL COLOR · 80 PAGES · $12.99 US / $16.99 CA · ISBN: 978-1-68405-155-7

IDW
WWW.IDWPUBLISHING.COM